The light was ... n was
hanging low i ... were
appearing over ... Kate
realized that tl ... l been
... constantly since the day the ... ed in, ...
... ce and cold. And now it ... Then, from
the other side of the hedge, they heard a scream.
Kate grabbed Mum's arm. The scream came again,
and she saw a soft white shape float away across
the field.

'An owl,' whispered Mum. 'A barn owl, I think . . .'

Green fingers

PAUL MAY

ILLUSTRATED BY
SIÂN BAILEY

CORGI YEARLING BOOKS

GREEN FINGERS
A CORGI YEARLING BOOK : 0 440 864569

First publication in Great Britain

PRINTING HISTORY
Corgi Yearling edition published 2002

1 3 5 7 9 10 8 6 4 2

Copyright © Paul May, 2002
Illustrations copyright © Siân Bailey, 2002

The right of Paul May to be identified as the author of this
work has been asserted in accordance with the
Copyright, Designs and Patents Act 1988.

Set in 13/15pt New Century Schoolbook by
Phoenix Typesetting, Ilkley, West Yorkshire

Corgi Books are published by Transworld Publishers,
61– 63 Uxbridge Road, London W5 5SA,
a division of The Random House Group Ltd,
in Australia by Random House Australia (Pty) Ltd,
20 Alfred Street, Milsons Point, Sydney, NSW 2061, Australia,
in New Zealand by Random House New Zealand Ltd,
18 Poland Road, Glenfield, Auckland 10, New Zealand
and in South Africa by Random House (Pty) Ltd,
Endulini, 5a Jubilee Road, Parktown 2193, South Africa

For Emily

Winter

Chapter 1

Kate and Mike sat in the back of the car. Emily was wedged between them, fast asleep, with her dirty old bit of sheet grasped tightly in her hand. Mum and Dad were arguing as usual. Kate stared at the house through the patch she had cleared in the steamed-up window.

'Look at the garden,' Dad was saying to Mum. 'You've always wanted a proper garden. Look at those apple trees.'

Kate would have laughed, but it wasn't funny. They might actually be forced to come and live here. It was the edge of the world: a wilderness of flat, bare fields and huge skies. A giant wind howled around the car, flinging the freezing January rain at the windows. The apple trees looked dead, and the so-called garden was a jungle of weeds. Dad was still going on.

'You have to admit, we could use the space. The kids could have their own rooms. And we can afford it with the money from the flat.'

'Just,' said Mum. 'Only just. And if we buy it, what then? Anyone would think you hadn't read the survey report. I never knew there *were* so many different kinds of rot. Then there's the damp, and the roof . . . and the drains.'

'Oh, come on,' said Dad. 'It's survived for three hundred years. It won't fall down tomorrow. These places were built to last.' Mum snorted. 'I'll do the work myself,' Dad went on. 'One thing at a time. It's what I've always wanted to do. I'll take it nice and slow. We can all help. We'll be doing something together again.'

'Yeah? There's about fifty jobs in the flat you never got round to. I can just see you up on that roof.'

'That's different,' said Dad. 'I'll have time when we move. No more rushing out of the house at seven o'clock every morning, slaving away making money for somebody else. I'll be off the treadmill, out of the rat race. It's only a couple of tiles, for God's sake.'

'And the rest.'

The broken tiles were high up on a steep mountainside of roof. Waterfalls of rain overflowed the gutters and splashed down the walls. The wind lashed at a few spindly snowdrops that were poking their heads through the tangled mat of uncut lawn in front of the house. Kate couldn't imagine *anyone* climbing up there, and definitely not Dad.

'We could afford the one we saw this morning,' Mum said. 'The one on the estate. It was a nice little house. And the school was just round the corner.'

'It was a *box*,' said Dad. 'There wasn't room to swing a cat. I want freedom. We're supposed to be starting again. You can *breathe* out here in the country. Why don't you take one more look at the garden?'

'I can see it from here,' said Mum. But then she sighed and opened the door. An icy blast sucked all the warm air out of the car and spattered Kate with rain. She watched Mum and Dad picking their way through the brambles. Dad pointed. Mum followed, shaking her head.

11

Kate looked at Mike, her brainy kid brother, but he was miles away as usual, buried in his book. She reached over into the front seat and turned the radio on. She searched through the channels, but all the stations were rubbish. Then Dad was back. He switched the radio off and looked at Mike and Kate.

'What do you think, you two?'

Kate said nothing. She looked out of the window at Mum, still standing in the rain, gazing from the house to the garden and back again.

Mike looked up from his book. 'I like it,' he said. 'I want the room with the floor that slopes. The one with the beam in the ceiling. It's like being on a ship.'

'How about you, Kate?' asked Dad, as Mum climbed back into the car, rain dripping from her hair.

'It doesn't matter what *I* think, does it? It won't make any difference. I don't know why you made me come.'

'You *do* know why,' said Mum. 'You have to visit your new school.' She looked at her watch. 'Speaking of which, we'd better go, or we'll be late.' She turned back to Kate. 'They were very nice when I came last month. I was impressed. They . . .'

'Yes,' said Kate. 'You told us before, remember?'

Dad might go on about new starts and fresh air and freedom, but Kate knew that this school was the *real* reason they were here. Mum seemed to think that it would be different from the ones in London. Unlike Mike, Kate had never been any good at school. She'd always hated it, right from the very first day. She could still remember it now. Mrs Dixon had told her to stop painting before she'd even finished her picture. Kate had emptied the red paint all over the teacher's white dress. She smiled, thinking about it, as Dad drove slowly along the narrow lanes.

Half a mile from the house they passed a low grey cottage. An old man stood outside the gate, the rain streaming off his hat. He stared at them as they passed: a blank, hostile gaze.

'Neighbourhood watch,' said Dad.

'I wouldn't fancy knocking on *his* door and trying to borrow a cup of sugar,' said Mum.

'Fertilizer,' muttered Kate.

'What's that?' asked Dad.

'It's just a name,' said Kate. 'There was a kid at school. He came from the country. That's what we called him.'

'Delightful,' said Mum. 'The sooner you're away from that place the better.'

Across the fields a round-towered church stood alone, encircled by a wall of crumbling grey flint. 'Look at the trees,' said Mike. 'They look like people.' Around them in the wide flatness the weird shapes of solitary trees stood black against the sky.

'They look dead,' said Kate, 'like everything else around here.'

They drove on for several miles until they came to a small town. A sign by the side of the road said 'Welcome to Ruddon'. They turned into a housing estate. 'See?' said Dad. 'Boxes, that's all they are. Might as well stay in London as move to one of these.'

'We'll talk about it later,' said Mum. She said that a lot. *Argue about it later*, she meant, thought Kate. *Fight about it later*. But Mum was still talking. 'This is what really matters,' she said, as they pulled into a car-park in front of a low brick building. The school. Kate felt her stomach churn.

'I'll stay here with Emily,' said Dad. Mum looked at him. 'Well we can't take her in, can we?' he said. 'You know what she's like when she's just woken up. And anyway, you're better at this kind of thing.'

Mum shook her head, annoyed. 'I'd just like a little support sometimes,' she said. Kate climbed out, hugging herself with goose-pimpled arms as the wind sliced through her thin T-shirt. Mum grabbed a coat from the

14

back seat. 'Put this on,' she said. 'You'll freeze.'

'I'm not cold,' said Kate.

'I don't know why I bother.' Mum threw the coat back into the car. Mike got out, and they all walked towards the entrance.

'Good luck, then,' Dad called after them.

The headteacher was friendly. Too friendly, thought Kate. Mike had been whisked off by a couple of boys for a tour of the school. Mum and Kate sat in the head's office. 'I'm Mrs Denby,' she said. 'It's lovely to meet you, Kate. I know you must be dying to look around, but I thought we should have a chat first. Get to know each other a little.'

Mrs Denby launched into a glowing description of the school. Kate stared out of the window at the ragged grey clouds that were chasing each other across the sky. Then she realized that the headteacher had stopped talking, and was looking at her expectantly. 'Well, Kate,' asked Mum, 'what do you think?'

Kate shrugged. 'Dunno,' she said. She sensed Mum bristling, trying to hold back her annoyance.

'I do understand how you feel, Kate,' Mrs Denby said. 'I know how hard this must be for you. Your mum told me that you've not been terribly happy at school.' Kate shot a furious

15

look at Mum, and then stared at the floor, wondering just how much Mum had said. 'Our school is different,' Mrs Denby continued. 'You *will* give us a chance, won't you, Kate?'

'Of course she will,' said Mum.

'We like to feel that this school has something for everyone. You'll have a real welcome here. We want *every* child to succeed. I know you've had trouble learning to read, Kate, but . . .'

'I don't *like* reading,' Kate burst out. 'So what? Everyone says it's a *problem*. That's all I am – a problem.'

'Kate!' said Mum.

'It's quite all right, Mrs Oakley. I think we should hear what Kate has to say.'

'What's the point? Nobody *listens* to me. Can we go now? Is that it?'

The headteacher stood up. Kate smiled to herself. Mrs Denby was trying to keep that calm, civilized expression on her face, but Kate could see she was finding it hard.

'One of our pupils will show you round the school, Kate, while I talk to your mother. I'm sure you'll feel differently when you've seen what we have to offer.'

'I doubt it,' muttered Kate, but Mrs Denby pretended not to hear. A tall, skinny, dark-haired girl was waiting outside.

'Ah, Louise,' Mrs Denby said, 'this is Kate Oakley. Kate may well be joining us after half-term. I'm sure you know what to do.'

'Yes, Mrs Denby.'

The headteacher turned and ushered Mum back inside her office. They were already deep in conversation. 'There are many new approaches, you know,' Mrs Denby was saying, 'and I can't help thinking that not all of them have been tried with Kate.'

The door closed. Kate stared at the other girl. She'd never seen anyone with such perfect school uniform before. The sweatshirt looked as if it had only been taken out of the packet that morning. It was a disgusting shade of orange. The words *Ruddon Community School* were written in a circle around a picture of a church and a tractor. She imagined what Suzy and Yasmin would say if they ever saw her wearing it. The girl was waiting. Kate followed her down the corridor.

'You from London, then?' Louise asked.

'What if I am?'

'You must be really fed up, having to move here.'

'We might not even *be* moving,' Kate said.

'I'm going to live in America when I leave school,' Louise continued. 'I can't wait to get out of this place.'

'Oh yeah?' muttered Kate.

Louise shrugged. She shoved a door open and said, 'Library.' They walked through. Several kids in orange tops were reading quietly. Down another corridor they came to the gym. Thirty kids in identical PE kit were playing a game. Louise swept on.

'Playground.'

'Field.'

'Art room.'

'Science labs.'

Everywhere, children in orange tops were working quietly. Like zombies, Kate thought, as Louise led her back to Mrs Denby's office. She stared at Louise's back. She didn't look like someone who was desperate to get out. She looked just like all the others.

'Excellent,' said Mrs Denby. 'Thank you, Louise. You two got on well then?' She didn't wait for an answer. 'I hope you'll carry on the good work, Louise, when Kate joins us. Make her welcome. Introduce her to your friends.'

'Sure,' said Louise. Kate looked at her. She was certain she had heard the faint twang of an American accent. Mrs Denby had heard it too. She looked sharply at Louise, but said nothing. She turned to Kate and smiled.

'I know it's hard, starting a new school,' she said, 'but I'm sure you'll enjoy yourself when you settle in.' Kate was about to reply, but Mum grasped her firmly by the arm.

'Thank you very much for your time,' she said to Mrs Denby, and Kate found herself being marched out of the building.

'How could you?' Kate demanded when they came out of the doors. 'Why did you tell them? You call that a fresh start?'

'Don't be stupid, Kate. They have your records. All anyone wants to do is *help* you.'

'And I'm supposed to be grateful? What else did you say to her?'

'We had a very useful discussion.'

'I bet!'

'You really don't do yourself any favours, do you? Mrs Denby wants to help. You could have been a bit more polite.'

'They're all the same. They won't be any different to the last lot.'

'Well, you tell me then. What are we supposed to do? Everybody does their best for you and this is all the thanks they get.'

'We don't have to move. If they're all the same I might as well stay where I am. At least I'd have my friends.'

'Exactly,' said Mum.

'Well?' asked Dad, as they got into the car. Emily was sitting on his knees pretending to drive. She clambered into the back seat and Kate strapped her in.

'Kate was her usual cheerful self,' said Mum, 'but I didn't see anything to make me change my mind.'

'Great!' said Dad. 'So what about Church Farm?'

'You're sure you can handle it? You're going to have all the kids to look after, remember? And all that work to do on the house.'

'Now, hold on a minute. I thought we'd decided . . .'

'We haven't *decided* anything,' said Mum. 'I said I'd take some time off when we move, and that's *all* I said.' Mum stared out through the rain-washed windscreen. 'I said I'd *look* for a job up here. But I haven't seen anything in the paper to make me feel optimistic.'

'Mum?' said Kate. 'I don't understand. What are you talking about?'

Mum hesitated. 'We weren't going to say anything yet,' she said, 'but I can't see there's any point in not telling you.' She looked at Dad. 'Well, Dave?'

'If you must,' said Dad.

'What?' demanded Kate. 'Tell us what?'

'Yeah, go on,' said Mike. 'What's all this about?'

'When we move,' said Mum, 'I may have to

keep on working in London, for a while at least.'

'But you can't!' Kate exclaimed. 'How can you?'

'I'd go to London on the train on a Monday morning,' said Mum. 'Lots of people do it. Kathy says I can stay at her place during the week. I'd be back in time for tea on Friday night.'

'But . . . but Dad said you haven't decided.' Kate couldn't believe this was happening.

'Dad thinks I might find a job here. But I really don't think that's very likely. Not a job as good as the one I've already got. Don't look like that, Kate. I'm not going to abandon you. If we buy this house then we're going to need some money coming in, at least until Dad gets his business sorted out. Anyone can see there's an awful lot of work to do . . .'

Dad turned suddenly to look at Mum. 'You think we should do it, then? Buy Church Farm?'

'It's obviously what you want,' said Mum. 'And there's the garden. It's a massive job, but if you're sure you can cope . . .'

'Yes!' exclaimed Dad and Mike together. Dad started the engine. 'We'll drive to the estate agents now,' he said. 'We'll put in an offer. Then it's pizzas all round to celebrate.'

Kate looked at Mike. How could he be *pleased*? Hadn't he heard what Mum had said? But now he was chattering away to Mum and Dad about how many football pitches they had at the school. And all Emily cared about was the pizza. Sometimes Kate thought that no-one cared about *her* at all.

Chapter 2

Kate picked her way carefully over the frozen mud towards the house. The postman didn't come to the door. He left the letters in a box by the roadside. Not that there were any for her. She could see the church tower, a few fields away, but there were no other houses in sight. Only windswept fields. Kate shuddered.

'Cold enough for you?' The old man stood in the road, shoulders hunched against the wind, a black trilby hat pulled down hard over his eyes. Kate looked up, and her trainer crunched through the frozen crust of a puddle into icy mud. The white Nike came out covered in black ooze. Kate swore. The old man coughed. Or maybe it was a laugh.

'You want boots for that.'

Kate ignored him and carried on towards the long, hump-backed building that was supposed to be her home. His scruffy black dog skittered over a sheet of ice. It nosed at her jeans, then it backed off, barking wildly. Kate froze. She was terrified of dogs.

'Tell it to stop. Get it out of our garden!'

'Garden!' said the old man. 'There was a garden there once. En't a garden now though, is it?'

'I don't care what you call it. Just get that dog away from me. It's going to bite me.' The dog lost interest suddenly, and wandered back towards the road. The old man coughed again.

'You don't want to worry about Pups,' he said. 'He won't hurt you.'

Kate had reached the front door. Split planks and peeling green paint. The man watched.

'Settling in all right, are you? Keeping warm?'

'We're fine, thanks,' Kate lied.

'That's been empty a fair while. The damp

gets right into the bones of an old place like that. Can't get rid of it.'

Kate listened in spite of herself. It was true, what he said. The house felt like a tomb. It was the end of February, and they had been there five days – the longest, coldest, most boring five days of Kate's life. The only good thing about it was that she wasn't at school. It was half-term.

She pushed the door. It was stuck again. She kicked the bottom savagely and it flew open. The old man was still watching. 'When do the builders start, then?' he asked.

'They don't. We're doing it ourselves.'

'You what?'

She slammed the door shut, and bent to take off the freezing trainer. At least that shut him up, she thought. She heard the old man shout at his dog as he walked away down the lane. What a nerve, poking his nose in, letting his dog run all over the place. Anyone could see it was savage.

The hot tap in the kitchen coughed, and a lump of water spat into the sink. The pipes began to shake and there was a distant clanking noise. No more water appeared. Mum stared at the tap in disbelief. 'Where's Dad?' she demanded.

Kate shrugged. 'I think he's doing something on the computer.'

'Well go and get him,' said Mum. 'Get him *now*.'

Dad jumped when Kate opened the door. The tiny room was beautifully warm; Emily was playing on the floor and a strange pattern shifted and grew on the computer screen.

'Mum wants you,' said Kate. 'I think the water pipes are going to explode. With any luck the whole stupid house is about to collapse. Then we can go home.'

'Rats!' said Dad. 'I was just getting started.' The patterns on the screen didn't look much like work to Kate, but she didn't say so.

'Shut the door,' Dad told her. 'I can't have that computer getting damp.'

Kate took Emily's hand and followed Dad through the house. Dad seemed a lot more worried about the computer than he was about the fact that the place was falling to pieces around them. Dad's list of things to fix grew every day. A lot of things got added, but nothing ever seemed to get crossed off. When Kate and Emily reached the kitchen, Mum was shouting.

'The beds are damp, the wind blows through the windows as if they weren't there. You put heaters on but they don't make any difference.

God knows what the bills will be like. The only warm room in the house is full of that flaming computer.'

'It's my living,' said Dad. 'Our living.'

'You wish,' said Mum. 'How much work have you had so far, then? After all those letters you sent out, and all those nights you stayed up before we moved, setting up the website? Go on, surprise me.'

'It's early days. Once the word gets around, there'll be loads of work.'

'Well, while you're waiting for it to flood in, maybe you could fix the taps. And then you can start on the rest of the list.'

The phone rang, and Emily ran to answer it. 'Hello,' she said. 'I'm Emily.' She listened. 'Mum. It's a lady. She wants to talk to you.'

Mum took the phone from Emily. 'Oh, Rachel. Hi. What . . . ?' There was a long pause while Mum listened. 'What, *now*? You mean today? But why?' Another pause. 'OK,' Mum said finally. 'If I leave now I can just about make it. No, don't worry.' She looked at Dad. 'It'll be a relief to get out of here for a few hours. No. I'll tell you all about it later.' Mum put the phone down. 'That was Rachel. My boss,' she said. 'There's a crisis at work, and they need me. I'm going in.'

'But you're on holiday,' said Dad. 'You're

seriously proposing to drive to London and back? I thought you were going to look for jobs today.'

Mum laughed and pointed at the paper. 'You look at those jobs in there. Look at the pay! It's not much more than half what I'm earning. I'd better go and change.'

They heard Mum's footsteps thudding up the stairs. Five minutes later she was back again dressed in her smart city clothes. She started rummaging through the jumble of old newspapers and breakfast things that covered the table, looking for the car keys. 'Come on,' she said. 'Help me, you lot.'

'I still don't see why . . .' began Dad.

'No,' cut in Mum. 'You wouldn't. Maybe you could fix the plumbing while I'm gone.' She kissed Emily and Mike.

'I'm coming, too,' said Kate suddenly. 'I can go and see Suzy and Yasmin.'

'Sorry, Kate,' said Mum. 'No time. It'll take me nearly three hours to get there, and I'll have to go straight to the office. I should be back just after six.' She gave Kate a quick hug. Kate looked up at her face. The phone call seemed to have brought her to life. Her eyes were sparkling. Mum was always like this when she had an important meeting at work.

They heard the car start, and the sound of the engine faded into the distance.

Kate glanced at Dad. His face looked as if it might crumple at any moment. Since they'd moved in, Mum and Dad had hardly been speaking. Dad had promised Mum that it would be a simple job to get the heating and the hot water working, but he'd been wrong. Mum had been grim-faced most of the time, and shivering. The arguments had been even worse than the ones they'd had in London. Somehow, Kate knew, things weren't right between Mum and Dad. It wasn't just the moving, or the house. Sometimes she wondered if things had ever been right. Mike was sitting at the table with his head in a book. It was OK for him, thought Kate. He could just pick up a book and the rest of the world ceased to exist.

'It's not fair!' she burst out. 'Mum knows how much I miss my friends. She should take me, too.'

'Listen,' said Dad, 'it's going to be tough for a while. We knew it would be. But it's going to be great. We've got space. We've got this fantastic house. It's going to take a bit of hard work, that's all. Then you'll love it. Mum'll love it too.'

'Oh, sure,' said Kate.

Dad ignored her. 'I guess I'd better make a start,' he said, tying his long hair back into a pony-tail and pulling on a pair of red overalls. 'Pass me that book will you, Kate?'

The do-it-yourself manual was brand new. It weighed a ton. It had a clasp on the front like a small suitcase. Dad couldn't get it open. Kate could see that his mind wasn't on what he was doing. She reached across the table and flipped the catch.

'Oh, right. Thanks. OK, let's see . . . Taps.'

'Hmmm,' he said, half an hour later. 'Sounds like an airlock. All we need is some hosepipe.'

'Are you sure you know what you're doing?' asked Kate.

'Easy,' said Dad. 'No problem. Just watch me.'

He went out of the back door and came back with a length of black tubing. 'I knew I'd seen some. Right – one end on the cold tap. One end on the hot. Turn them all on, and Bob's your uncle!' There was a gurgle from somewhere above them, then silence.

'How long do you do it for?' asked Kate.

'Might as well make sure,' said Dad. 'Blast all the air out of the system. Don't want it . . .'

He was interrupted by a yell – Mike's voice.

'Hey! What's going on? There's water coming through the ceiling.'

Dad ran up the stairs, two at a time. In Mike's room, water dripped steadily onto the bed. Mike was staring helplessly at the sagging ceiling.

'Don't just stand there!' Dad cried. 'Move the bed. We'll never get it dry.'

'Don't you think you ought to do something about the water?' said Kate. 'Would you like me to turn the taps off?'

'Oh, my God!' said Dad, shoving Kate out of the way. 'How's that?' he yelled up the stairs. The water continued to rain down. After a few minutes it became clear that it wasn't going to stop.

'The stop-cock,' said Dad. 'We have to find the stop-cock.'

'It's in the bathroom,' said Kate. 'Behind the sink. I think we need a plumber.'

Mum arrived home as the plumber was leaving. He was shaking his head. It was an interesting head, Kate thought. Bright pink with a green stripe down the middle. He'd spent hours figuring out the complicated tangle of pipes that ran through the house.

'What's going on?' asked Mum.

'This is Marty,' said Dad. 'He's a plumber.'

31

'Oh,' said Mum. 'You've seen sense at last.' Kate could see Mum's eyes flickering to Marty's hair and the ring that pierced his bottom lip.

'It was raining *indoors*!' cried Emily, her eyes shining with the memory.

'What?' said Mum.

'It's OK,' said Dad. 'Don't worry.'

'That's a big old job you've got on here,' the plumber said. 'I've sorted out something temporary. And I've showed Mr Oakley here what he needs to do.'

As Marty moved to one side to pick up his bag of tools, Mum saw the 'temporary arrangement'. Two pipes rose out of the floor with taps on top, like antennae on some weird insect. There was an orange washing-up bowl underneath them.

'It's not that difficult,' Dad was saying. 'Once Marty explained it to me, I could see how simple it was. It'll take a bit of time, that's all. But it'll save us a fortune if I do the work.'

Marty took one look at the expression on Mum's face, and headed for the door. 'See you, kids,' he said. 'Bye, Mr Oakley, Mrs Oakley. I left my card. If you need me . . .'

'That's typical,' said Mum. 'When you do see reason and call in a plumber, you end up with a cowboy.'

'He's nice,' said Kate. 'We all like him.' And it was true. Marty had been fun. He'd been cheerful. He'd made it seem as if doing up the house was actually possible.

'And he's a good plumber,' added Dad.

'Huh,' said Mum. She pointed to the taps. 'That's good plumbing, is it? I don't think so, Dave. Why can't you face facts? We're going to need professionals to sort this place out, and that's going to cost money.'

'I don't want to talk about it now,' said Dad.

But Mum didn't stop. 'I'm *glad* I went in to work today,' she said. 'It made me realize that I'd be mad to give up my job. I told them they didn't need to worry. I told them I was staying on.'

'You did what?' Dad was angrier than Kate had ever seen him. The anger scared her. 'Without even *discussing* it? I thought you weren't going to decide until you'd finished your holiday.'

'Some *holiday*,' said Mum. 'You mean you were hoping I'd change my mind. Well, I'm sorry. They wanted to know what my plans were and I told them.'

Kate felt Emily clinging onto her leg. She picked her up and cuddled her. Emily put her fingers in her mouth. Kate wished *she* had an old bit of blanket to cuddle. Mike picked his book up from the table and went out of the room.

Kate's head swam. Mum was saying something else, but it didn't make sense. 'What?' Kate said.

Mum reached across the table and took her hand. 'Listen, love, I really am sorry,' she said. 'I wish it didn't have to be like this, but it looks like I'll have to go in to work on Monday. In fact, all next week.'

'But . . . but we start school on Monday,' stammered Kate, 'and it's Emily's first day at Nursery.'

Dad just stared. 'You can't,' he said.

'If there was any way I could avoid it, I would. I feel awful, but two people left suddenly this week. If I don't help them out I'm not sure I'll still have a job to go to.' Mum turned to Kate. 'I won't miss your first morning at school,' she said. 'I'll catch a late train on Monday, so I'll . . .'

Kate stood up. She opened her mouth to shout at Mum, but then she saw Emily's worried face looking up at her. She took a deep breath, and choked back the angry words. 'It's OK, Mum,' she said finally. 'Don't worry about me. I'll be fine. Absolutely fine.' And then she went quickly out of the room, before Mum or Dad or Emily could see her tears.

Chapter 3

'You! New girl! Pay attention!'

Kate jerked herself back to the present. The geography teacher was standing at the front of the class, pointing to a whiteboard covered with untidy writing and diagrams.

'Do you have the faintest idea what I've been talking about?'

Kate shrugged. 'Not really,' she said.

'Not really, *sir*!'

'Not really, sir,' Kate muttered. The teacher looked at her sharply. Then he carried on. Kate glanced around the room. Thirty kids in orange sweatshirts. She couldn't believe she was wearing one herself. At least she'd managed to sneak her trainers out of the house in the confusion. She was just waiting for one of the teachers to spot them. This one was still droning on. Kate found herself thinking about Mum and Dad. They had argued all Saturday night. Kate and Mike had listened outside the door . . .

'So what do you want me to do first?' Dad asked angrily. 'Sort the plumbing? Get my business up and running? Look after the kids?'

'You don't *have* to do the house yourself,' replied Mum. 'For crying out loud, that's the whole point! I'll earn the money and you can pay someone else to do it. Preferably someone with just the one colour hair and a bit less metalwork in his face. Preferably someone who knows what he's doing. And stop acting as if we'd never discussed it. You just didn't want to listen, that's all.'

'Marty's OK,' said Dad. 'Who cares what he looks like? We'd probably all be under water by now if it wasn't for him.'

'And we wouldn't have had the problem in the first place if it hadn't been for *you*.'

'But I *want* to do it myself. I'll learn. We've only just started. I thought we were going to do it together. You never give me a chance.'

'Oh, come off it,' Mum retorted. 'I've given you hundreds of chances. I'm being practical. That's something you've never understood.'

Then Dad said something else that Kate couldn't make out, and there was a long silence. When the voices began again, they were too quiet to hear. Kate turned to Mike, but he'd gone.

This morning, Mum had shaken her awake gently at 6.30. She'd heard the bedside light click on, and felt Mum's weight on the bed, felt her hand stroking her hair. Kate sat up in bed and hugged Mum, as if she was four years old again. As if she had never been to school.

'I know it's hard,' Mum said. 'It's hard for all of us. But this time school will be different.'

'Don't go to London, Mum.'

'I have to, love. I know it's not perfect, but I'm sure it's the best thing.'

Kate couldn't find anything to say.

'You'd better get up now. But you will promise me? You'll try at school?'

Kate bit her lip. Why was it that the one thing that Mum wanted from her was the one thing she couldn't give her? Why was school the only thing that seemed to matter?

Kate had *tried* before. *Trying* didn't make any difference.

She remembered how pleased Mum had been when she had brought her first reading book home from school. She had always loved the picture books Mum read her at bedtime. She'd never bothered about the black squiggles at the bottom of the pages. But now, suddenly, the squiggles had seemed to be the only important things. Kate had brought the same book home, night after night, trying to remember what she was supposed to say. And still the black squiggles had made no sense. Finally, she had taken a fat black felt tip and scrawled all over the words and pictures. Mrs Dixon had asked Mum to come in and see her. Kate could still remember Mum's red, embarrassed face.

'OK,' she said at last. 'I'll try.' She picked up the orange sweatshirt that Mum had bought her when they were visiting the school. 'Do I really have to wear this?' she asked.

But Mum was staring out of the window. 'I suppose the garden will have to wait,' she said, almost to herself. Kate went and stood beside her. The sky was brightening in the east, and they could just make out the ragged shapes of the bushes and trees emerging from the darkness.

'When I was a kid, I always wanted a garden,' Mum said softly. 'We went out for the day once, from London, when I was tiny. It must have been to visit some friend of Mum's and Dad's. We sat at a table in the garden. It was hot, and there were cakes and ice-cream. And then they sent me off to play. I can remember the green everywhere, and the sunshine, and the coolness under the bushes.'

'Not like this, then,' Kate muttered.

'Well, it could be. Who knows?'

Kate looked at Mum. She was hardly ever like this these days. A lot of the time she seemed hard and angry. Kate peered down into the tangled mess below them as the light grew stronger, trying to imagine a lawn and a table, and flowers. It was impossible.

'Look at the time!' Mum headed for the door. 'We'd better get moving.'

Kate stared at herself in the mirror. Just another orange zombie. Then she grinned – and popped the Nikes into her bag.

Mum looked cool and businesslike as she stood outside the school gate, dressed in her sharp city clothes. Dad stood beside her, wearing his old jeans with the holes in them, and a paint-covered jumper. Mum looked as if she belonged to another world. Emily was running round in circles. She was so excited about going to Nursery that she couldn't stand still. Kate wished she felt the same way. Mike had already been snatched up by a bunch of boys on the playground.

'It's OK,' Kate said. 'You can leave me here. I'll be fine.'

'If you're sure,' said Dad. Kate could see that he was desperate to go. Dad hated schools. He always looked as if he was worried that he was going to get in trouble for something.

Mum smiled and kissed her. 'I *know* you're going to be OK,' she said. 'We'd better be off, before Emily explodes.'

'Are we going to Nursery *now*?' asked Emily, standing still for a second.

'Right now,' said Dad. 'Say goodbye to Kate.'

Emily flung her arms around Kate and hugged her really tight. Kate blinked back her tears. She waved as they walked away, but she couldn't speak. She stood for a moment, wondering where to go, and then she heard a voice.

'Hi. I'm supposed to look after you.'

It was Louise. She must have been waiting. A bunch of kids were clustered on the other side of the playground, watching them.

'Who are they?' asked Kate.

'Don't worry about them. I'll show you where to go.'

'I wasn't worried. I just wondered.'

'Come on,' said Louise. 'We're in Miss Peters' class. She doesn't like people being late.'

'Hang on,' Kate replied. 'I need the loo.'

Two minutes later, she emerged wearing the trainers. Louise looked at them, but didn't say anything. She led the way to the classroom.

And now the geography lesson was over and the teacher had noticed the trainers. Kate felt a familiar thrill of excitement.

'You! New girl!'

Kate turned. 'My name's Kate, sir. Kate Oakley.'

Long years of practice had helped Kate to perfect her way of talking to teachers. Almost polite. Almost rude. Nothing definitely wrong that they could do you for. This bloke thought he was on to a winner with the trainers though. 'What are *they*?' he said. 'On your feet.'

'Trainers, sir.'

'Trainers are forbidden. Detention.'

'But, sir, it's my first day. And we've just moved and everything's still packed up and Mum couldn't find my school shoes and we didn't have time to buy any.' Kate watched the teacher hesitate. 'I'll try and find my school shoes tonight, sir,' she said.

'Make sure you do.' Kate felt a glow of satisfaction. The teacher was still talking, but he was backing down, blustering. 'I don't know about your last school, but I should warn you that we take uniform seriously here. If I see those trainers again there'll be trouble.'

Outside in the corridor several kids were waiting.

'Great!' said one – a tall boy with red hair and a goofy grin.

'Brilliant!'

'Cool!'

Kate was surrounded by kids, laughing and joking. 'No-one's got away with that before,' said the red-haired boy.

'Kate?' Louise butted in. 'I have to show you the Study Centre. You'll be late.'

'Oooohh!' said one of the others. 'I bet you're really scared, aren't you, Kate?'

'Forget about *her*,' said the redhead, looking at Louise. 'I'm going there myself. That's 'cos I'm thick.' They all laughed. 'Come on. Follow me.'

The boy's name was Brian. 'What you doing with that Louise, then?' he asked as they walked across a courtyard.

'Nothing. Someone's told her to show me round, that's all.'

'She's well snooty, she is. Stuck-up boff. No-one likes her.'

Kate got the message. Stay clear of Louise or they wouldn't like her either. She bristled.

'Yeah, well,' she said, 'I haven't made my mind up yet.'

'What you in here for anyway?' Brian asked her, as if it was a prison they were going to.

'What do you mean?'

'Well I'm in here for being thick, right? And some people are here 'cos they're a bit funny in the head. So how about you?'

'Why don't you just tell me where to go,' said Kate, 'before I lose my temper?'

Brian opened his mouth as if he was going to say something else. Then he thought better of it. 'You'd better see Cartwright,' he told her. He pointed down the corridor, and then opened the door beside him. A lot of noise came out, and a teacher shouted, then the door closed.

Kate walked to the end of the corridor. The plate on the door said *Mrs Cartwright*. She thought suddenly of Yasmin and Suzy. No-one would ever have called *them* thick. Dangerous, maybe. Bad, maybe. But not thick. Brian seemed to think it was cool to be stupid. And she wondered what Louise had done to upset them all so much. She knocked on the door and went in. The teacher stood up to meet her.

'Kate? I'm Mrs Cartwright. We'll be seeing quite a lot of each other, I expect.'

Kate gazed at the shelves. The games and puzzles stacked there were like old enemies. They'd been boring her stupid since she was seven years old.

'I think we'd better take a look at just where you're up to with your reading,' Mrs Cartwright said, producing a stack of forms from her desk. 'I'd like you to read me a few pieces from my little book.'

Kate felt herself reddening. She had been through all of this so many times before. She felt angry words rising to her lips, and then she remembered Mum, standing at the window, gazing into the garden, asking her to try. She stopped herself somehow. Winding up the teachers was one thing. Losing her temper was different. Kate sat down and began to read, halting and stumbling over the words.

After school, Louise showed her where to catch the bus. Kate ignored the funny looks from some of the other kids. She'd make her own mind up about Louise. 'I catch this one too,' Louise told her. 'You must live near me.'

Kate heard a yell, and saw Mike. He was

kicking a ball around with some other boys. He waved at her.

'Who's that?' Louise asked.

'My brother,' said Kate. 'Ignore him. The village is called Eastfield.'

'Next to mine,' said Louise. 'That's where my grandad lives.'

'Has he got a savage dog called Pups? And a hat?'

'You've met him, then. The dog's not really savage. Just a bit pig-headed. Like Grandad.' Kate looked at Louise as the bus rumbled through the countryside. She couldn't fit her together, somehow, with the old man.

'This is where I get off,' said Louise, a few minutes later. There were no houses anywhere in sight. Just flat brown fields with no hedges. A concrete track ran, straight as an arrow, across the fields. Kate watched Louise climb down and begin walking off slowly into the distance. The bus was empty now, apart from Mike. He lurched down the aisle and dumped himself in the seat that Louise had left.

'How'd it go, then?' he asked.

Kate shrugged. 'It's a school, isn't it?'

'Only asking. You friends with that girl, then?'

'I don't know,' said Kate. 'I don't know what to think.'

45

* * *

The bus stopped right outside the grey cottages. As it pulled away a dog began to bark, and the old man's black hat appeared over the hedge.

'Thought I might see you,' he said. 'You get some schooling these days.'

Kate stopped and looked at him. His face was amazingly brown, as if he'd just spent six months in Majorca. 'Didn't you go to school, then?' she asked.

'Not a lot. Left when I was fourteen. Had to go to work, see?'

'You went to work when you were *fourteen*?'

'Started before that. Never went to school at harvest. Or when there was hoeing to do.'

'But your mum and dad . . .'

'That was Dad wouldn't let me go. Waste of time, he said, when there was work wanted doing.'

Kate stared at the old man. He had to be making it up. He was grinning at her, and suddenly began to cough. For a moment he couldn't get his breath. 'Are you OK?' she asked.

'En't nothing wrong with me,' said the old man sharply, when he had recovered. 'I hear you had a bit of trouble with the plumbing,' he went on. 'You tell your dad, if he need any help, just ask Walter. That's me.'

Kate laughed. Dad was hopeless, but it was hard to see how an old man could help him. She was wondering how he had heard about the plumbing when he said, 'What do they call you, then?'

'I'm Kate,' she said, 'and this is Mike. We'd better go now. Mum'll be wondering where we are.' And then she remembered. Mum wasn't there. Mum was in London. Kate was suddenly anxious about Emily. 'D'you think she really understood,' she said to Mike as they walked along the lane, 'about Mum not being here?'

'I bet she'll be fine,' said Mike. 'She loves helping Dad, and I bet she had a great time at Nursery.'

Just for a second, Kate heard something in Mike's voice that made her pause. It was almost as if he was worried himself. But that was ridiculous. Then Mike was off, dribbling a pebble along the road. Kate shook her head. She'd imagined it. Mike loved it here. He had loads of friends already. And he never worried about anything.

When they got home, Emily was having a great time. Dad was feeding her a baked-bean-and-poached-egg sandwich, and they had to listen to the complete story of her first morning at Nursery. It was only much later, when they were all in bed, that Emily appeared in the doorway of Kate's room. The wind had risen again, and was loud in the treetops outside. 'I don't like the noises,' Emily whispered. 'Can I sleep in here with you?'

Kate lifted the edge of her duvet. Emily climbed in beside her and closed her eyes. Kate lay awake for a while, listening to the wild night outside, thinking of Mum, miles away in London. Then she put an arm around Emily, and fell asleep.

March late winter
early Spring

fragrant cream
flowers
Lonicera fragrantissima

Chapter 4

Kate went to school. She went every day. She told herself that she went to school because there was nowhere else to go. Ruddon was the deadest dump she had ever seen and Norwich was twenty miles away. She'd thought about bunking off and going there on the bus, then discovered that there was only one bus a week, and that was on a Saturday. She'd almost forgotten what a city was like. And at least school was a distraction from what was going on at home. School was normal. It was just what you'd expect school

51

to be. At home everything was strange, and getting stranger.

It was a Friday afternoon at the end of March, and Kate had already survived five whole weeks of school. She was following Mike slowly along the lane on the way home from the bus-stop. As soon as they turned the corner she saw the small figure perched on top of a pile of bricks.

'Emily!' she yelled. 'What's happened?'

'Bang!' Emily shouted, waving her arms in the air. 'Crash!' Emily was black from head to foot. Kate sniffed at her. Soot.

There was rubbish everywhere in the front garden. Dad had spent the last five weeks ripping out plaster and rotten wood, wallpaper and broken tiles. Every day there seemed to be less of the house inside, and more of it piled up in the garden. Dad appeared in the doorway. 'Come and see,' he said. 'It's unbelievable!'

It wasn't the fact that Mum was only here at the weekends that was so weird. That almost seemed normal now. Monday mornings were horrible, but now Friday nights were extra special – something to look forward to. Only, things between Mum and Dad just seemed to keep getting worse. Dad stubbornly refused to do what Mum wanted him to do. On Friday nights, when Mum arrived home, it was brilliant to see her, but it never took long for the rows to begin again.

Kate looked at Dad. He was smiling, but his face was thin and drawn. His eyes were bright, but they looked like the eyes of someone with a fever. They followed him into the living room. The fireplace had gone. The room was full of blackened bricks. There was a hole in the wall like a cave. Stalactites of wallpaper hung around the edges.

'Where's the TV?' asked Kate.

'Forget the TV,' said Dad. 'Look up there.'

Kate poked her head into the gap. The chimney was massive. You could have driven a car up it. She could see a small square of sky far above her.

'Mum's going to love this,' Mike said, gazing around the room. 'You'll never clean this lot up before she gets back.'

Dad stared at him. 'It's not Friday, is it? What's the time?'

'Nearly five,' said Mike. 'You can't leave it like this, Dad.'

'No,' said Dad. 'I suppose you're right. You'd better give me a hand. Mike, you get the wheelbarrow. Kate, there's a pair of gloves over there.'

'Oh, great,' said Kate, but she pulled the

gloves on. Then a thought struck her.

'You haven't made the tea either, have you?' she said. Dad dropped the brick he was holding. It fell on his foot. Kate picked it up while he hopped around the room. 'You'd better go and do the cooking,' she told him. 'We'll sort this lot out.'

They removed the bricks and swept up as well as they could, then they dragged the chairs and the TV back into the room. A gale was blowing down the chimney. When she plugged in the TV and tried to watch *Beech Grove*, Kate discovered that Dad had sliced through the aerial cable. Now they didn't even have a TV. She stormed into the kitchen.

'How could you?' she yelled at him. 'The TV was just about the only normal thing in the whole house, and now you've wrecked that too.'

Dad was frying onions and garlic with one hand while he tried to chop up more vegetables with the other. He ignored her.

'You're ruining everything,' said Kate.

'Oh, yes?' Dad threw a handful of chopped chillies into the pan and they all started to cough. He looked away from the cooker, wiping his eyes. Then he stared at the children. 'Look at the state of you,' he said. 'Mike! Your hands are black! If you want a quiet weekend, you go and clean up. Come here, Em. I'll give you a wash and we'll go and fetch Mum. You two clear up in here while we're gone.'

When Kate and Mike returned to the kitchen, Dad and Emily had disappeared. There was a good smell coming from the oven. She heard the car start. At least he wasn't going to be late. But the kitchen . . .

Kate looked around, seeing it as she knew Mum would see it. The walls were bare, crumbling brick. There was no plaster on the ceiling. If you were in Kate's bedroom, you could see straight through between the floorboards into the kitchen below. A single lightbulb hung by a tattered wire from the ceiling, and Marty's temporary sink was still there – two taps and a plastic bowl. The cooker, the washing-machine, and the camping table and chairs stood around the room looking as if they'd just been beamed in from outer space. Every week Mum pinned up a list of things for Dad to do. Every week the sink was at the top of the list. Every week Dad looked at the list and then did something different.

And now his mess was everywhere. Dad claimed that he cooked in a creative frenzy. He left a trail of devastation behind him. Dirty pans, carrot tops, onion skins, empty tins. 'You sweep the floor,' she said Mike. 'I'll deal with this lot.' She had only just finished sorting everything out when she heard the car.

Dad walked in with Emily, and he didn't even notice what they'd done. His face was red and angry as he bent to look in the oven. Kate went to find Mum. She was in the garden, staring at the latest pile of bricks. 'It's such a mess,' Mum said. 'Such an awful rotten mess. Why can't he . . . ? Oh, never mind. Let's have a look round the back.'

Kate glanced up at Mum's face. She looked pale and tired. 'Are you OK?' she asked.

Mum sniffed. 'Of course I am. Exhausted, that's all. And I did kind of hope . . .' She stopped. 'How about you? How's school?'

'OK,' said Kate. Mum looked at her. 'Well, I haven't bunked off, have I? I've been every single day. You know I have.'

'And?'

'It's a school, isn't it? That's all.'

They walked on in silence. The light was fading fast, and a thin moon was hanging low in the sky. The first stars were appearing overhead. Everything was still. Kate realized that the wind had dropped. It had been blowing constantly since the day they moved in, fierce and cold. And now it was gone. Then, from the other side of the hedge, they heard a scream. Kate grabbed Mum's arm. The scream came again, and she saw a soft white shape float away across the field.

'An owl,' whispered Mum. 'A barn owl, I think. I never knew they made a noise like that, did you?'

Kate shook her head. She looked around her. The house loomed above them, black against the deepening blue. A star pricked out behind the chimney, and the light glowed from the upstairs windows. It didn't seem real.

'Hey!' said Mum. 'Smell this!'

A tangle of branches was blocking their way. Mum pulled one down and waved it under Kate's nose. The branch was covered with tiny white flowers that gave off a sharp, clean scent. 'There *must* have been a garden here once,' she said. 'Someone planted this.'

They stood together for a moment. 'Oh, well,' Mum sighed. 'I suppose I'd better take a look inside.'

When Mum walked into the kitchen and saw that the sink still wasn't there, Kate thought she was going to cry. 'I know, I know,' said Dad. 'But honestly, you won't believe what I've found next door. Come on.' He led the way into the living room. The lightbulb swung from the ceiling in the cold draught that came from the chimney. It lit up the brickdust and soot that still clung to every surface. Mum scooped Emily up into her arms.

'There,' said Dad. 'Look!'

Mum didn't burst into tears. Kate could see she didn't want to upset Emily. Instead, she said, 'Oh.' Then she looked up the chimney. She stood in it and shouted. Her voice echoed and Emily laughed.

'You like it, then?' asked Dad. 'I reckon it's seventeenth-century.'

'Right,' said Mum. 'Great. And when are you going to start on the kitchen?'

'Tomorrow,' said Dad. 'I've got all the stuff. I thought you could help.'

Kate looked from Mum to Dad and felt the tension crackle between them.

'Come on,' said Mum. 'Let's go and have tea.'

Cosmos

Chapter 5

The next morning, Kate was woken by dazzling sunlight. Dad had pulled back the curtains. She looked at her clock. It was ridiculously early. 'What's going on?' she demanded.

'Kitchen sink,' said Dad. 'I have to start now, so I can get it finished by tea-time. I'm turning all the water off in exactly fifteen minutes, so get washed and have some breakfast.'

'Probably be the last wash we have for weeks,' Kate said as she dragged herself out of bed and stared at the cardboard boxes that held all her possessions.

'Have a little faith. Marty showed me what I had to do. It's simple. And anyway, Mum's helping.'

'Yeah?' Kate looked at Dad. Obviously he'd done some kind of deal with Mum. He looked very pleased with himself. In the kitchen, Mum was filling containers with water – buckets, bowls, saucepans.

'We won't need them,' said Dad, leafing through the do-it-yourself manual. 'I told you, we'll have the water back on in time for tea.'

'Look,' said Mum. 'I'm helping. OK? I'm not sure why. It's not exactly the relaxing weekend I had in mind, but I'm doing it. And if something goes wrong . . .'

'It won't,' said Dad. But Mum went on filling containers. When she had finished, she pulled on a pair of overalls and Dad turned the water off. Then he started to unscrew the cold tap. A fine spray of water filled the air.

'Don't worry,' said Dad. 'It's just a build-up of pressure. As soon as I get this off . . .' He wrenched with the giant spanner. The spray turned into a small fountain.

'Stop it!' screamed Mum.

'I don't understand,' muttered Dad. 'Marty said . . .'

'I don't care what Marty said. Make it stop.'

Dad turned and ran upstairs.

'I want to splash, too,' said Emily, and she dipped her hands in the nearest bucket.

'Get her out of here,' said Mum, between gritted teeth. 'My God, this is just so *typical!*'

'But where?' asked Kate.

'I don't care,' said Mum. She was trying to stop the water by holding her hand over the tap. It wasn't working. 'Anywhere! Just go!'

They stood in the lane outside the house. The sun was shining and it was almost warm. In London they could have gone to the park, or the shops, or round Yasmin's house. Kate stared at the fields. Flat. Dead. No street-lights, no cars, no houses, no people.

'What about the church?' Mike offered. 'We could go there. Have a look in the graveyard. See if there's any ghosts.'

'You don't see ghosts in the daytime, stupid.'

'What ghosts?' asked Emily.

'There aren't any,' Kate told her, with an angry glance at Mike. Ever since Mum had gone back to work, Emily had been worrying about noises in the night. Most mornings, Kate awoke to find Emily asleep beside her.

They set off down the lane, but they never reached the church. They had just passed the grey cottage when Emily yelled, 'Cows!' She started pulling at Mike's hand. 'Look! Lots of cows!'

Three enormous black and white animals had appeared in the road, and were heading towards them. More appeared, and then more. Emily kept laughing and jumping up and down, but it wasn't funny. There were thick, high hedges on both sides of them.

'We'll have to run,' Kate said. 'Come on, quick!'

'I want to see the cows,' said Emily. She was about to start crying.

'You *have* seen them,' said Kate. 'If you stay here, they'll squash you.'

'I want to see the *cows*,' Emily repeated. Kate got hold of her hand and started trying to drag her along the road, back the way they had come. It was hopeless. Emily went red in the face. She screamed and screamed. Mike was useless. He stood in the road, laughing. Then Kate heard a voice.

'You don't want to be scared of them. Stand still. They'll go round you.' The old man was looking over the hedge at them. Walter. Louise was beside him.

'Grandad's right,' she said. 'They won't hurt you.'

'How do *you* know?' Kate demanded. 'There are hundreds of them.'

'No there aren't. There are eighty-seven. They're my dad's.'

The eighty-seven cows were getting nearer, and Emily was still screaming.

'Why don't you help us?' yelled Kate. Walter laughed. He walked over and opened the gate. Instantly, the dog was there beside him, barking. Walter grabbed his collar, and Kate edged nervously past.

'Come you in, and shut it behind you,' Walter said. 'I don't want them in here.'

'I thought you said they were harmless.'

'They don't eat children, anyhow,' Walter grinned. 'But they'd make a proper mess of my vegetables. And they have done, before now.'

Kate looked at the garden. It was nothing but bare earth, all the way from the front gate to the house. 'What vegetables?' she asked.

'Don't get him started,' Louise said. 'Grandad's not even supposed to do gardening. Are you, Grandad? You know what Mum says. You should get your veg from the supermarket like everyone else.' She took the dog from Walter and tied him up by his kennel.

'That don't taste of nothing,' said Walter. 'There's no guts in it.' He picked up a hoe and walked off down the path.

Louise shrugged her shoulders. 'You can't tell him,' she said.

'You were laughing at us,' Kate accused her.

'Well, you did look funny. I mean, everyone knows about the cows.'

'Well, *I* don't.'

'No,' said Louise. 'I can see that. Is this your sister?' Kate nodded.

'*She's* not scared of cows, anyway,' said Louise. Emily was still peering through the bars of the gate. Mike was almost as fascinated as Emily was. Louise picked Emily up just as the biggest cow of the lot ambled towards the hedge.

'Hey!' Kate shouted. 'What are you doing?'

'Don't panic,' laughed Louise, as the cow put her head on top of the hedge and started scratching the loose folds under her chin on the thorny twigs. 'This is number twenty-eight. I've known her since she was a baby. She always comes to see me if I'm here. Look.' Louise reached out and grabbed the cow's ear. There was a yellow label fixed to it. Twenty-eight. Suddenly the cow flicked out a huge pink tongue and licked Emily's ear. Emily squeaked with pleasure. 'Again!' she yelled.

Kate turned away. She couldn't help it – the cows terrified her. She stared at the black soil that stretched all the way to the house. Walter was scratching in the earth with the hoe. He looked up, then he beckoned her over.

'Here,' he said. 'Look.'

Kate walked down the path. Anything was better than cows. She stared at the black mud.

'Well?' said Walter. Kate crouched down. And then she saw. There were tiny plants there, hundreds of them, so tiny that at first you couldn't see them at all. They were in neat rows, running across the garden.

'What are they?' she asked.

'Parsnips, this lot.' He bent awkwardly and pointed to the nearest row. 'Then there's carrots, spinach. All sorts.'

'What were you doing to them? With the hoe?'

'Stopping the weeds,' said Walter. 'Stirring 'em up, see? Before they get the chance to grow.'

'Leave her alone, Grandad,' said Louise. The cows had gone, but Emily was still clutching Louise's hand. 'She's not interested in all that stuff.'

Kate saw the old man's face change as he stood up. 'You used to help me,' he said to Louise. 'You liked it then. Too much schooling, that's your trouble.'

'Oh, come on, Grandad. Don't start.' She turned to Kate. 'Grandad thinks I should be out in the fields, hoeing the sugar beet, don't you, Grandad?'

'Ah, well, said Walter. 'You think I don't

mean it, but that wouldn't do you no harm. Get your head out of them books once in a while. Just you wait there. I've got something for Debbie.'

'That's Mum,' Louise told them, as they watched Walter walk over to a complicated arrangement of old bricks with rotting window frames balanced on top of them. He lifted a frame and propped it up with an old flower-pot. Then he reached inside and stood up holding two lettuces. 'First this year,' he said proudly. He gave one to Louise.

'Grandad! You know Mum won't . . . Well, anyway, I can't take it like this. It's all dirty. Haven't you got a bag?'

'I en't a blooming shopkeeper,' Walter muttered. 'You know where to find one.' Louise disappeared inside the cottage. Walter offered the other lettuce to Kate. 'Here,' he said. 'For *your* mum. Or are *you* scared of a bit of dirt, too?'

Kate took the lettuce. It was damp and cold. 'Not dirt,' she said. 'Just cows. And dogs.' She put the lettuce down on the path and picked up the hoe. 'Can I have a go at this?' she asked. The wooden handle was polished smooth. It felt comfortable. The handle was long, maybe half a metre taller than she was, and at the end was a curved metal blade. She lifted the blade to look at it more closely.

'Careful!' exclaimed Walter, as she reached out a finger towards the gleaming silver edge. 'That's sharp! Look.' He pulled a piece of paper from his pocket and sliced it neatly in half.

'Sharper than our kitchen knife,' said Kate. 'What do I have to do?' She dug the blade into the surface and pulled gently.

'Go on,' said Walter. 'Don't be scared of it.'

Kate tugged harder, and the hoe ran quickly along beneath the soil, like a small earthquake.

'That's it. Now you walk along the row, and mind those parsnips.'

Very slowly, Kate made her way across the garden. After a few metres she stopped and leaned on the hoe. A robin fluttered down onto the newly turned earth, pecking quickly at something Kate couldn't see. Louise came out of the cottage and said something to Mike.

'Come on, Kate,' called Mike. 'Let's go.'

Kate paused. 'You go,' she said. 'I'll catch you up. I'll see you at the church.'

She watched the others leave, Emily swinging happily between Mike and Louise as they went out of the gate. The robin flew up to sit on a fencepost. It put its head on one side. It seemed to be watching the blade of the hoe slice through the damp earth. Kate had never noticed before how strong the earth smelled. Before she knew it, she was at the end of the row. She straightened up. Her back was stiff, and she was sweating. Her arms ached.

'Had enough, then?' called Walter. Kate shook her head, turned, and began to work her way back across the garden. 'You're a sticker,' said Walter, when she reached the path again. 'I'll give you that.'

Kate stood the hoe against the fence. Her hands were sore. Blisters had appeared on her palms.

'Harder'n it looks, en't it?' Walter said. He wasn't laughing now. His voice was kind. 'You keep at it and maybe one day you'll have hands like mine.' He held out his own hands, palms upwards. They were brown and hard. The lines on them looked as if they had been carved into wood. 'Green fingers, see?' he said. 'Maybe you got 'em too. I could give you a few plants, if you like. Come you round here.'

He led the way round the side of the house. There was even more garden at the back, and big plants were growing there. 'Broccoli,' he said, waving at some things that looked like overgrown cabbages covered with netting. 'Have to keep the pigeons off,' he said, 'or they scoff the lot.'

On a bench by the side of a small greenhouse there were some trays full of tiny plants. Walter lifted one to show her. 'See here,' he said. 'These are too close together now. I was just pricking them out. Giving them room to breathe. You can do a few for yourself.'

He showed her how to tease the delicate, overcrowded plants apart from each other, and settle each one into its place in a new tray. Kate held a miniature leaf gently between two fingers and looked at the white root, not much thicker than a strand of hair.

'What are they?' she asked. 'How big do they get?'

'*Cosmos*, they're called,' said Walter. 'My missus loved 'em. They'll be as tall as you are. Taller. Here, look. You keep this.' He handed her the seed packet. The picture showed a mass of big pink flowers, like giant daisies. Kate looked at the scrap of green between her fingers. It didn't seem possible.

'I haven't even got anywhere to put them,' she said, as she walked down the path with a small tray of plants in one hand and a lettuce in the other.

'Can't put 'em outside yet anyway,' said Walter. 'Not till the end of May. Frost'll kill 'em. Keep 'em on a window-sill. Plenty of time to dig a patch for 'em.' Then he coughed. He took a deep breath, and coughed again.

'You ought to sit down,' said Kate.

'En't nothing wrong with me.' He picked up the hoe.

Kate looked back as she went out of the gate. The old man was working his way doggedly along the next row. The robin sat on the fence and watched him.

Chapter 6

The churchyard was an island completely surrounded by fields. There was a low wall around it, made from flints. The church was made from flints too: lumpy grey stones with white stuff jammed between them. Three twisted trees stood at one end of the graveyard. Kate followed a narrow path from the lane, and pushed open the heavy wooden gate. Louise was sitting on a gravestone, watching Mike and Emily explore.

'Hey!' called Mike. 'It's your name, Louise! You are called Fuller, aren't you?'

Emily had climbed onto a big stone slab. Mike was pointing to the words that were carved in it. *'Nathaniel Fuller,'* he read. *'Born 1735. Died 1801. Also his beloved wife Mary. The Lord is my shepherd.'*

The letters were almost worn away. Grey and orange lichen was creeping over them. This was a game Kate couldn't play. She glanced at the words on the stone, and then looked away, feeling herself flush. Everywhere you went, words followed you around. You couldn't get away from them. Mike started scrambling from stone to stone. 'Here, too!' he yelled. 'Edward Fuller. Another Nathaniel. Elizabeth.'

Louise stood up. 'My family,' she said. 'They're all buried here. They never went anywhere. Just stayed here in this place. Can you imagine?' She looked around at the flat, empty fields. 'Look over here. That's my grandma. Grandad's wife.'

There was a small stone and a vase with fresh red flowers in it. Mike read the words. *'Margaret Fuller. Beloved wife of Walter, Mother of Edward and Lucy.'*

'Grandma died last year,' Louise said. 'Grandad was miserable for ages. He's still grumpy now. Well, you saw him. He brings flowers every week. He grows them in his greenhouse. Edward's my dad and Lucy's my auntie. She lives in California. We went to visit them last summer. It was just brilliant. You lot must be crazy to move to a place like this.'

'I like it here,' said Mike.

'Well, I'm getting out,' said Louise. 'You've seen them at school. You can see what it's like round here. That's why Grandad snaps at me the way he does. I think he secretly hoped I'd be a farmer. Now I've seen America, I know that's where I want to go. It's so big. And this place is so small.'

Mike asked her some question and she was off again, babbling about the USA. Kate wandered away with Emily. Round the back of the church, out of the wind, it was warm. Almost hot. The grass was soft and green with little flowers growing in it. Kate sat down with her back against the lumpy church wall and felt the sun on her face. She heard Emily's voice say, 'Louise!' Kate opened her eyes, but Louise wasn't there. Emily was standing by a gravestone. 'Louise!' she said again.

'Yeah, yeah,' Kate told her. Emily was always playing at reading and writing. She'd been so desperate to start at Nursery. A fat lot *she* knew. Kate looked at the stone. Emily was pointing at the words. 'That's not *Louise*,' Kate said. 'Even I know that. It says *Fuller*.'

73

She stopped, surprised at herself. She knew the word said *Fuller*. As soon as she saw it, a picture came into her mind – Louise's face. Kate sat there in the sun, thinking about it while Emily played. There were other words like that. Words that had pictures and feelings to go with them. Words like *Mum* and *Dad*. But most words just slipped away from her like water. Words with no pictures, no feelings. Kate hated those words. The more she looked at them – and she had looked at them a lot with one despairing teacher after another – the more they melted into one another.

Louise and Mike came round the side of the church.

'We're going to Louise's now,' Mike said. 'She's got some brilliant games. And she's got four controllers. We can all play together.'

'Really, it's not that great at my place,' Louise said. 'Can't we go to yours?'

Kate stood up, wondering what was going on at home. Better to stay away. Better not to think about it. 'Not a good idea,' she said. 'Dad's playing with the plumbing again. We'd probably all drown.'

Louise climbed over a stile in a corner of the churchyard, and headed off through the middle of a field.

'Hey!' said Kate. 'There are things growing.'

It was like Walter's garden. From a distance the field had looked brown. But now she was standing in it, Kate could see millions of tiny shoots pushing up out of the earth. 'We can't walk across here,' she said. 'What if the farmer sees us?'

'I told you,' said Louise. 'The farmer's my dad. And anyway, it's a footpath. Look.'

A sign pointed like a finger into the middle of nowhere. This didn't look like any footpath Kate had ever seen. In fact, as far as she could make out, there was no path at all. Louise simply trampled on the plants. The field seemed to go on for ever. When they were right in the middle of it, Kate felt as if she was at sea. Nothing but field all around them.

'There's my house,' said Louise. 'Over there.'

They looked where she was pointing. There were several enormous metal buildings like giant dustbins, and beside them a big square house, all raw red brick and dazzling white windows.

'I thought it would be old,' Kate said. 'I thought you told me your family had lived here for hundreds of years.'

'Didn't you know?' said Louise. 'We used to live where you live now. Church Farm. Mum couldn't stand it. I don't see how you can. It's falling down, isn't it?'

'No it's not,' said Mike fiercely. 'It's brilliant.' Kate didn't say anything.

'Mum!' yelled Louise, leading them into a porch the size of a garage. 'I've brought some friends. You'd better take your shoes off,' she told them.

Kate looked in through the back door. The kitchen was vast. Surfaces gleamed. The floor was spotless. Kate wondered what to do with her lettuce. It was dripping soil onto the floor. And she was still holding the tray of tiny plants in her other hand. Then Louise's mum appeared.

'This is Kate,' said Louise. 'And Mike and Emily. They've moved into Church Farm. We rescued them from the cows.'

Louise's mum looked harassed, thought Kate. She saw Mrs Fuller's eyes glancing at their feet, and felt glad that they'd taken off their shoes.

'Well,' Mrs Fuller asked Louise, 'what did he say?' Louise's face fell.

'I'm sorry, Mum. I forgot.'

'Louise! That was the only reason you went. Now I'll have to send Dad. Well come in, then,' she said irritably to the rest of them. Then she spotted Kate's lettuce and her tray of plants. 'I think you'd better leave them outside,' she said.

'He sent one for you, too,' Kate told her. She had almost decided that she didn't like Mrs Fuller. Mrs Fuller sighed, took the carrier bag from Louise, and put it on the gleaming worksurface. 'The sooner we get him into that home, the better,' she said. 'I wouldn't mind all the fetching and carrying if he'd just be sensible. But no. He has to have a garden the size of a field.'

They sat uncomfortably round a big table and Louise gave them glasses of Coke. She put the glasses on little mats. While they sipped at their drinks, Mrs Fuller interrogated them. At least, it felt that way to Kate. She wanted to know all about Mum and Dad. About where they had lived before. About school. Mike did all the talking. Kate sat there, wishing she hadn't come, looking around at the dull emptiness of the kitchen. Then she heard what Mrs Fuller was saying.

'And as for bringing *children* to live in that awful old place. What does your mother think? I suppose it was your father's idea.'

'It's not awful,' said Kate hotly. 'And it was everyone's idea, moving here. We like it.' Kate pretended not to see Mike's astonished stare. She was surprised at herself. Maybe it was the fine weather that had come at last. She remembered the sweet smell of the flowers in the darkening garden, and the owl, and the stars.

'Dad's mending the house,' said Emily. 'He's making it all better.' Kate and Mike both laughed. Then Kate saw that both Louise and Mrs Fuller were looking at them all as if they were slightly crazy. That only made her giggle more. She tried not to look at Mike. He was red in the face and looked as if he was about to burst.

'Hmm,' said Louise's mum. 'And how are you settling in to your new school?'

'OK,' said Kate.

'You're very lucky to be able to go there,' Mrs Fuller said. 'It has an excellent reputation. Louise is doing extremely well there. All her teachers say she's going to go on to university eventually, and we hope . . .'

'Mum!' Louise was pink with embarrassment.

'Well, it's the truth, isn't it?' Mrs Fuller said, picking up the empty glasses. 'Being clever is nothing to be ashamed of, Louise.' As she bent to put the glasses in the dishwasher, the back door opened. A tall man with a red face and untidy hair stood there, smiling. He took a couple of steps inside the door.

'You found some friends, then, Louise,' he said. 'That's great. Who . . . ?'

'Ted!' exclaimed Louise's mum. 'Your boots! Get out of here! I've just cleaned the floor. You think I haven't got enough to do already?'

Mr Fuller looked down at his boots. They were covered with mud.

'You're just like your father,' said Mrs Fuller. 'Never think about the trouble you cause other people.'

'I thought we could go upstairs,' said Louise. 'Is that all right? They want a go on my Playstation.'

'One hour,' said Mrs Fuller. 'Then you need to start on your history project.'

Louise led the way to her bedroom. Kate felt she had to walk on tiptoe. In the hallway there was thick clear plastic stuff laid over the carpet to stop it wearing out. Everything in the house looked new. It looked as if nobody ever touched anything. Louise's bedroom was easily the tidiest bedroom Kate had ever seen. There was a special desk for the computer, the TV and the video. The bookshelves were crammed full of books, but there were none on the floor or on the bed. In Mike's room you couldn't move without treading on a book. Louise bent to take the Playstation from a cupboard where it sat neatly on a shelf. She handed it to Mike, with the extra controllers. Kate noticed that they were in boxes, as if they had never been used. Then Louise saw what Emily was doing. Emily could never resist bouncing on beds – and Louise's bed was very bouncy. The smooth white cover slid to the floor with a muddy mark across it. Some dirt always clung to Emily, even when you thought she was clean. Louise was paralysed with horror.

'You can't!' she gasped, dumping Emily back on the floor and brushing at the muddy mark. She put the cover back on the bed and smoothed it out carefully.

'Can I read a book?' said Emily. She began to pull books from the shelves.

'Stop her!' Louise was panicking.

'Haven't you got any of your old toys?' Kate asked. 'Lego? Anything like that. Emily likes to be doing something.'

'I can see that,' Louise said, as Emily grabbed the bedspread and started to pull it off the bed again, 'but it's no good. All my old toys are in the attic.'

'We'd better go,' Kate said, 'before Emily does something really bad.'

'No, don't,' said Louise. 'Please.'

Kate looked at Louise. She should have realized before. Louise was miserable. No brothers or sisters. All alone in this spotless house. She had a Playstation with four controllers and no-one to play with. On the wall there was a cork noticeboard. Louise actually had her homework timetable pinned up.

'OK,' said Mike, who had been looking through the games. 'We're ready. Hey! Brilliant! You've got *Flying Gorillas*. Come on, Emily. You can play too.'

That did the trick. Playing a real game with big kids was exciting enough to keep Emily sitting in one place for almost an hour, squeaking with excitement as her gorilla hurtled through space.

'What did you forget to do?' Kate asked Louise as they were leaving. 'Why was your mum so fed up?'

'We're taking Grandad to visit a home this afternoon,' Louise replied. 'If Mum and Dad can make him get into the car, that is. We've taken him to visit four so far. He's hated them all.'

'Louise is OK, isn't she?' Mike said as they tramped back across the endless field.

'I wasn't sure at first. The kids at school can't stand her, but that's just because she's clever. Now I've seen her house – and her mum. It's like she's a prisoner. Look at that place!'

The farm buildings were black against the sky. There was no garden around the house, only grass and concrete. Kate found herself looking forward to getting home.

But even before they reached the gate, they could hear Mum's voice. She was yelling at Dad. Something had gone badly wrong. Kate looked at Mike. He shrugged and opened the door. There were pipes and water everywhere. The new sink unit was propped up on a kind of frame and Dad was standing beside it with three pieces of pipe in his hand.

'They gave me the wrong bit,' he was saying. 'It's not my fault.'

'It never is though, is it,' Mum shouted. 'If you'd done this last week when you were supposed to . . . Now the shops are closed and we won't have any water until Monday. And then it'll be something else, won't it? There's always something.'

Kate felt Emily's hand squeezing hers tightly. 'It's not the end of the world,' Dad said, trying to calm Mum down. 'You can't expect things to be straightforward all the time.'

'*Some* of the time would be a start,' said Mum. 'I suppose I should be glad I filled up these pans. I can't take much more of this, Dave. I just can't.'

Mum turned round and saw the children. Before she could hide it, Kate saw her eyes fill with tears. Then she rushed out of the room.

Chapter 7

Mum spent Sunday morning clearing up. Dad was in the computer room. Working, he said. There was a frozen silence between him and Mum that scared Kate. She found the hoover, and spent most of the morning using it. Then, after lunch, Mum said, 'Homework.'

'Why can't you help Mike?' Kate grumbled, as Mum followed her into her room.

'Mike doesn't need help,' Mum replied. 'You do. Show me.'

Kate tipped up her school bag and dumped the contents in a heap on the table. Mum glanced at her sharply and then picked up the homework diary. 'OK,' she said 'spellings first. You'd better sit here and practise them. I'll come back in ten minutes.'

Kate stared at the list of words. If learning spellings was *that* easy, she would have learned them years ago. Like Mike. Even Emily would be able to do it. The list of words in the dog-eared book blurred and drifted away. Kate gazed out over the tangled garden to the wide fields and the wider sky. The fields were as flat as ever, but they were changing. There was a faint mist of green over the brown. Things were growing. Kate looked over at the little plants in the tray on the window-sill. This morning she had found new leaves beginning to grow. She'd have to think about where she was going to dig.

'What *are* you doing, Kate? What's your teacher going to say about that? Look at it.'

Drawings of tiny plants covered the spelling book. Mum carefully tore out the pages. 'There. With any luck they won't notice. Sometimes I think you just don't want to learn anything. I thought you told me school was OK.'

'Well, it is,' Kate said. 'You haven't had any letters, have you? Or phone calls.'

Mum shook her head. 'I suppose you must be

doing something right,' she agreed. 'Now let me help you with these. See if you can't get them all right tomorrow.'

Kate watched Mum as she wrote the words on the page. Her face was hard, tight. An image filled her mind suddenly: Mum standing outside in the darkness as the owl flew by; the smell of the white flowers.

'Mum,' she said, 'you know the garden? Why don't we start? I could help you.'

'You have to do *this*, Kate. This is what matters.' Mum looked at Kate's face and put the pen down. 'Look, Kate, it's a nice idea, but there simply isn't time.'

'But there is,' said Kate. 'It's light in the evenings now, so there's Friday nights when you get back. And all day Saturday and Sunday.'

'I'm sorry,' said Mum. She hesitated.

Kate turned, sensing something wrong. 'Mum?'

'I . . . there aren't going to be any weekends. Not for a while.'

Kate stared at her. 'What do you mean? Mum?'

'I need some time, Kate. Time on my own.'

Kate felt dizzy. The floor didn't seem solid. 'You and Dad,' she began. 'You're not . . .'

'Don't ask me that, Kate. Not now. But it's

no good, me and Dad fighting like this all the time.'

'Then *don't*,' said Kate.

'Oh, Kate,' Mum put her arm around her. 'I wish it was that easy.'

'But what about *us*?' Kate said. 'What about me and Mike and Emily. It's not just Dad, is it? You can't just *leave* us.'

Tears were streaming down Mum's face. She stood up and walked to the window. 'I'm *not* leaving you,' she said. 'But I've got to have time, Kate. It's all such a mess. I have to sort things out in my head. I'm so sorry. About everything.'

Kate went and stood beside her. Mum stroked her hair. 'It'll be all right,' she whispered. 'It'll be all right in the end.'

It didn't feel all right to Kate. The rest of the day passed in a blur. She wanted to scream and yell at Mum and Dad – tell them not to do this. But they hadn't told Mike, not everything anyway. Just that Mum was working next weekend. And they hadn't told Emily either, of course. So, with Mike and Emily, Kate was supposed to pretend everything was normal. She was still pretending the following morning, when Mum came with them to the school gates.

'You'll be late for work,' Mike said. He had

been very quiet since Mum had told him she had to work next weekend. Mum put an arm around him and kissed the top of his head.

'Mum!' he said, looking around anxiously to make sure none of his friends were watching. 'What are you doing that for?'

Mum looked up, and Kate found herself looking directly into her eyes. She felt her heart lurch. She felt Mum pleading with her, and she knew what she had to do. Everything was normal. Nothing was out of the ordinary. 'Have a good week at work, Mum,' she said, trying to stop her voice from shaking.

Mum bent and kissed her. Dad looked at his watch. 'We'd better go,' he said. 'You'll miss your train.'

Kate watched as Mum strapped Emily back into her seat. She watched her pale face, as she waved through the car window. She watched until she couldn't see the car any more. She felt like crying, but she knew she couldn't. She turned and walked into the school and saw Mike still standing there. 'Well?' she snapped. 'What are you staring at?'

She walked past him and across the playground, seeing nothing.

The first lesson was geography.

'We're starting a new unit today,' said Mr

Grahame. 'For the next three weeks, we shall be studying Kenya. I suppose it's too much to hope that any of you will know where Kenya is? Well?' Kate raised her hand. So did several others. Mr Grahame's eyes lit briefly on Kate's face, then slid past her. 'Matthew?'

'Africa, sir?'

'Correct. Well done, Matthew. But Africa is a big place. More detail, anyone?' Kate looked at the teacher's pompous face, at the little bristly moustache on his top lip. He wouldn't ask *her* if she was the only person in the class. She felt the anger building inside her. She *liked* the feeling. She had almost forgotten what it was like.

'Jenny?'

'North Africa, sir?'

Kate had had enough. 'It's in *East* Africa,' she said scornfully. 'The capital is Nairobi. There are big game reserves with lots of elephants. It has . . .'

'I beg your pardon. Did I ask you to speak, young lady?'

'I know about Kenya,' said Kate. 'They don't. You should have asked me.'

'And maybe I would have done . . .'

'No, you wouldn't.' Kate hardly knew what she was saying now, she was so angry. 'You wouldn't have asked me because you think I'm stupid. You're all the same.'

Some of the other kids were laughing out loud now, and wondering what Mr Grahame was going to do. They didn't have to wait long. Mr Grahame's neck turned red.

'Get out!' he shouted, pointing to the door. 'Get out of here. You can wait in the corridor.'

'Sir.' It was Louise's voice. 'Please, sir, she did know the answer, didn't she?'

'Do you want to go out, too?'

'I don't think you're being fair.'

Mr Grahame stared at Louise. The whole class stared at her. Kate couldn't believe it. The other kids had all had a good laugh when she wound up the teachers, but none of them had ever joined in, or backed her up. And now Louise – the perfect pupil . . .

'See me after the lesson, Louise,' Mr Grahame said finally. 'And you.' He pointed a finger at Kate. 'Get out.'

Kate walked to the door and slammed it behind her. The corridor was empty. There was no way she was going to stand here for another thirty minutes. Her mind was racing. All this time – five whole weeks she'd put up with it and not lost her temper. But it had been good. Almost worth waiting for. And Louise! She would never have expected Louise to do that. Then, as suddenly as it had arrived, the anger was gone. She felt weak and sick. The corridor seemed to lurch and sway so that she clung to the wall. She needed air. She started walking. At the far end of the corridor, she opened a door and stared across the carpark. She sucked in the cold air and felt the sun on her face.

'And why aren't you in lessons?'

The voice belonged to Mrs Denby. The headteacher.

'It wasn't my fault,' Kate said. 'I was only trying to answer a question. But he wouldn't listen.'

'*Who* wouldn't listen?'

'Mr Grahame. He just ignored me.'

'And you were the soul of politeness, I suppose.'

'I lost my temper,' said Kate. 'I couldn't help it. I just . . .'

'Come with me,' said Mrs Denby. 'We'll go to my office. I don't want to stand about chatting in a draughty corridor.' They walked past the room where Mr Grahame was teaching. Mrs Denby opened the door. 'I'm taking Kate to my room,' she said. 'I'll talk to you later.'

'Frankly,' said Mrs Denby when they reached her office, 'I'm surprised this hasn't happened before. You came with quite a reputation. But you've obviously been making an effort.' The headteacher paused. She waited for Kate to say something, but Kate couldn't think what to say. Mrs Denby looked down at a sheet of paper she had taken from the filing cabinet. 'You haven't thrown any chairs. You haven't smashed any windows. And you have been attending school regularly.'

Yes, Kate thought, remembering. She had done those things at her last school. It didn't seem possible. She could picture the classroom – the chair flying through the air. She shivered. It was like a scene remembered from a film.

Mrs Denby was still talking. 'We'll overlook this incident,' she said, 'but it mustn't happen again. Apologize to Mr Grahame, and we'll put it behind us.'

Kate still felt weak and shaken. She didn't have the heart for a fight. She nodded, and Mrs Denby led the way back to the classroom. Everyone was writing, but Kate knew that nobody would miss a word.

'Kate has something to say to you,' Mrs Denby told Mr Grahame.

'I'm sorry,' Kate said.

'Oh, are you indeed? And why are you sorry?'

Kate glanced at Mrs Denby. The head-teacher was looking at Mr Grahame. She didn't look pleased. 'I'm sorry I was rude,' said Kate.

'Yes,' said Mr Grahame, 'you were. Insolent is the word I'd use. I'm a little surprised to find that you haven't been sent home in disgrace.'

'I have spoken to Kate,' said Mrs Denby. 'This won't happen again.'

'Fine,' said Mr Grahame. 'Go back to your seat and get on with your work.'

'But I don't know what the work is.'

Mr Grahame was about to say something when he caught Mrs Denby's eye. He sighed loudly. 'Ask Louise Fuller,' he said. 'Go.'

Kate sat in her place copying a map of Kenya into her book. At least it was something she could do. Then the lesson ended. As Kate was heading for the door, Mr Grahame called her back. Louise was already standing by the desk.

'I suppose you thought you'd got away with it? Saying sorry makes everything better? Not so, I'm afraid. Detention tonight, please.'

The teacher turned back to his pile of books. Kate stared at the bald patch on the top of his head for a second. She was about to argue when Louise said, 'You can't do that, sir.'

'I beg your pardon?' The teacher looked up, obviously not sure he had heard correctly.

'I said you can't do that.'

'Don't,' Kate said, tugging at Louise's arm. 'You don't have to . . .'

'I don't know how it has happened,' said Mr Grahame, 'but you have obviously come under the influence of this troublemaker, Louise. Very disappointing. You can join her in detention. And I shall telephone your parents. They'll be very disappointed, no doubt. Now get out of my sight, both of you.'

Chapter 8

'You shouldn't have done it,' said Kate. 'It didn't make any difference. It's just got you in trouble too.' Kate and Louise were in the churchyard. They had caught the late bus after detention, and neither of them was in a hurry to get home.

'He made me angry,' said Louise. 'I've been watching, ever since you came. He made up his mind you were thick, and that's how he treats you. I didn't think he should get away with it.'

'Yeah, well he's wrong. And thanks.'

'I know.' They were at the door of the church:

94

a low rounded arch of carved stone. 'Have you been inside?' Louise asked.

'Can you?'

'Sure. It's not locked.' Louise lifted the latch and pushed the heavy oak door. Kate had expected darkness, but everything inside was light. She had only been in a church once before, for Grandad's funeral in a grimy building in a London back street. Hardly any light had filtered through the gloomy stained-glass windows. Here, the sun flooded in through tall, pointed arches. The walls were white, and even the pale timbers of the roof and pews seemed to have been bleached by the light.

'It's fantastic,' said Kate. 'I had no idea.'

'I come here sometimes,' said Louise. 'If I get fed up with Mum. If I want to think. Hardly anyone ever comes here apart from me.'

'What will your mum say, then?' asked Kate. 'When she finds out about today?'

'I don't know. It's never happened before. But I don't care. I was right. What about *your* mum?'

'She won't say anything. She's gone.'

The two girls stood in silence, looking at each other. Kate couldn't believe what she'd said. She hadn't meant to say it.

'I . . . I don't understand.'

'Mum would never have wanted to move if it hadn't been for me. She wouldn't.' Kate felt tears welling up in her eyes. She brushed them away angrily. 'We would have stayed in London and everything would have been all right. But now she's gone back to London and we're all stuck up here and it's my fault. She's gone.'

'That can't be right,' Louise said, after another long silence. 'It's *not* all because of you. You just *think* it is. Your dad wanted to live in the country. You said so. And your mum *likes* it here. It's just that she likes her job, too. That's what you told me. Well? Didn't you?'

Kate didn't say anything, but she could feel a strength in Louise that she hadn't noticed before. She was glad she had told her.

'You won't tell anyone else, will you,' she said, 'about Mum, I mean?'

'Who would I tell? No-one even talks to me.'

Kate looked at her. *'I'm* talking to you, aren't I?'

They sat for a while, neither of them speaking. The shadows and sunlight played on the walls. Birds were singing outside in the churchyard. Then Louise stood up. 'I told you this was a good place,' she said. She opened the door and they went outside. The sun was low in the sky now, and orange light slanted across the churchyard, casting long shadows. Smoke was rising from the chimney of Walter's cottage.

'Oh, no!' said Kate, remembering. 'I said I'd go and see your grandad. I told him I'd help with the hoeing.'

'Mum wouldn't think that was helping,' said Louise. 'She'd say you were encouraging him.'

'As far as I can see,' Kate said, 'he does exactly what he wants. If I'm quick I can still do a little bit. Are you coming?'

'I . . . I don't know,' said Louise. 'I'm late already. Mum's going to be mad enough as it is.'

'Anyone would think you didn't *like* going round there.'

'I do. Of course I do. I just hate the way he goes on at me sometimes, that's all. About how I do too much schoolwork.'

'But he's right, isn't he? No-one needs to work as hard as you do.'

'I want to, OK? If I don't I'll be stuck here for ever.'

'So it's not because your mum forces you?'

'She's stressed out, that's all. About Grandad mainly. I mean, it's embarrassing when she tells everyone how clever I am and everything, but I know it's only because she's pleased. I don't work because she makes me. I do it for me.'

Kate wasn't convinced. 'So you're not coming, then?'

Louise looked at her. 'I always used to help Grandad. It's just, after Gran died, he got quite ill. Everyone says he shouldn't be doing all that hoeing and digging. They say it's too much.'

'But he loves his garden. What would he do if he didn't do gardening? He'd probably be like *my* grandad was. Sitting in a room in a home watching TV all day long. And then one day he won't be there any more.'

'I suppose . . .'

'You know I'm right.' Kate pulled the door of the church shut behind them. 'Why don't you come? Just for a few minutes.'

Louise hesitated, then nodded. 'I did used to love it,' she said. 'We used to go on outings on Sundays. Me and Gran and Grandad. We always went to big houses, but we never went inside. We just walked round the gardens, looking at flowers. I can still remember the names of them . . . And I remember when I was *really* small, in Grandad's garden . . . there were flowers everywhere.'

'But there aren't any flowers. Only the ones in the greenhouse.'

'I don't mean here. Not in the cottage. In his

98

old garden. The one he made for Gran at Church Farm.'

'At *our* house?'

'I know it doesn't look like it now . . .'

'Hold on,' said Kate. 'I don't understand. I thought it was *you* who lived in our house. And your mum and dad. Not Walter.'

'Yeah. But we didn't live there for long. Before that, Gran and Grandad lived there. Grandad retired and Mum and Dad took over the farm. That was when I was five. But Mum hated it so we moved. The house has been empty ever since.'

'Then there really was a garden there? You actually saw it?'

'I was very little. I don't remember much. Just the flowers, and playing on the grass.'

'He might have said.'

'Grandad was angry about it,' Louise explained. 'He made the garden for Gran. It took him years. But then Mum and Dad let it get all overgrown, and when we moved out he couldn't bear to go back there.'

An idea leaped into Kate's mind. It was so obvious she didn't know why she hadn't thought of it before. She could uncover the garden herself. There was no reason why not. She knew how much having a garden meant to Mum. Maybe . . .

'There's a picture on Grandad's wall,' said Louise, 'if you're interested. I'm surprised he hasn't shown you before now.'

When they reached the cottage, Walter wasn't in the garden. Louise knocked on the back door. After a few moments they heard the sound of a chair scraping and then the door opened. Walter's hair was tousled and he was rubbing his eyes. 'Just having forty winks before tea,' he said.

'Grandad!' gasped Louise, 'What's that smell?' She rushed inside and emerged seconds later clutching a smoking saucepan.

'I was going to have some soup,' said Walter. 'I must have dropped off. No harm done. Would you like a cuppa? I'll put the kettle on.'

'I'll do it,' said Louise shortly. For a second she sounded just like her mum.

'What have you done with that saucepan?' Walter asked.

'It's in the bin,' said Louise. 'It was ruined.'

'That was my favourite, that was. You fetch that back.'

'You should be more careful,' Louise said sternly. 'You know what Mum would say.'

'Well, you'd better not tell her then, had you?' said Walter. 'Because the only way you'll get me into one of them places is to drag me in by the heels.'

'Grandad didn't like the home we took him to see,' Louise told Kate.

'They was playing cards,' said Walter suddenly, 'them as weren't asleep. "How about a bit of a bet?" I says. Trying to spice things up a bit, see? "We en't allowed," they says. Just like school, that was.' He began to cough.

'OK, Grandad,' said Louise. 'Calm down.'

'Walter,' said Kate, 'Louise says you've got a photo of the garden. The one at Church Farm. At our house.'

Walter pointed. On the wall behind Kate there was a photograph in a frame. The colours were so faded it was hard to tell if it was really a colour photo at all. There were four people in the picture. A man and a woman sat by a table in a garden full of flowers. Two children were playing on a rug on the grass beside the table. There was an old house in the background. Kate's house. She stood up to look more closely. The man was about Dad's age, maybe a little older; very brown and smiling. The woman was pouring tea.

'That's Maggie,' said Walter.

'And the children are Dad and Aunt Lucy,' said Louise.

Kate barely heard them. She was staring at

the garden. She could see paths in the picture. Paths made with huge flagstones. And there was a terrace of some kind. And low walls around the edge of the lawn. The background was a mist of faded flowers. The garden looked as if it might go on for ever. It must all be buried. But surely it would still be there! She said the words out loud. 'It's still there,' she whispered. 'Under all the weeds and the mess. It's still there, I bet.'

Walter looked at her. 'Of course it is,' he said. 'There's plenty of things buried under the ground. Whole villages. Why d'you think there's that great old church over there and hardly any houses? They're under the ground, that's why. You can't bring 'em back.'

But Kate hardly noticed the bitterness in Walter's voice. 'It's what Mum wanted,' she continued. 'I know it is. A garden like that. Just like that. And it's all there. I could do it. I know I could.'

Louise had been watching Kate, listening and thinking. 'I could help you,' she said suddenly. 'You'll need help. It'll be like one of those TV programmes where they turn a rubbish heap into a garden in a weekend.'

Walter started to laugh, and the laughter turned quickly into a fit of coughing. When he'd recovered, he looked at Louise, at her perfect uniform. 'You'll get dirty, you know,' he said. 'I don't reckon your mother'll be too pleased.' Then he started laughing again. Kate and Louise looked at each other and they both started laughing too. Kate felt as if she hadn't laughed properly for a long time.

'I'll tell you another thing,' said Walter. 'You won't do that in a weekend. And that'll be hard work. But I reckon I can help. I wrote it all down, you know. Every plant I ever planted. I drew plans.' He started to get up, and then he turned pale and sat back in his chair.

'Grandad,' said Louise. 'What's the matter?'

And then the door opened. Louise's mum stood there, her face cold, angry and worried all at the same time. 'I might have known,' she said. 'I had a phone call, Louise. From school. I couldn't believe it.' She turned to Kate, who was holding Walter's hand. 'You can get out of here, young lady,' she said. 'I don't want to see you with Louise again. And you can stay away from Dad, too. You've caused nothing but trouble.'

Kate hesitated for a second, then walked past her, out of the door, with tears stinging her eyes.

Chapter 9

'I've done it!' Dad exclaimed as Kate opened the door. He picked up the do-it-yourself manual and kissed it, then he grabbed Kate and whirled her round the room. 'Look!' he said. 'Admire!'

Hot and cold water were gushing into a shining, stainless-steel sink. The kitchen was full of steam, and the floor was covered in pieces of left-over piping. There was water everywhere. Mike and Emily were clapping. Dad took a bow as Kate looked for a dry surface to put her school bag down. Then he saw her face. 'Hey! Kate!' he said. 'What's up?'

'Nothing,' said Kate, and she ran upstairs to her room. Dad turned off the taps and followed her.

'It's school, isn't it? They rang me, but . . .'

'It wasn't my fault!'

'Did I say it was? As it happens I thought the guy sounded like a pompous idiot.'

'He is.'

'Yeah, well, after I talked to him I rang the head . . .'

'Dad!'

'Don't worry. I was polite. I was expecting her to give me an earful, but she didn't. You've done your detention, she said, so forget about it.'

Kate went to the window and stared down into the garden. Dad's words didn't mean a thing. School was *nothing*. She gazed at the dim shapes of the buried walls and flowerbeds. She blinked back the tears. 'I want Mum,' she said.

Dad put his arm around her shoulders and hugged her silently.

When he had gone, Kate began to think about the garden. If Dad could fix the plumbing on his own, then *surely* she could fix the garden. At least she had seen what it used to look like. But there was no chance of Louise or Walter helping her now. She'd have to do it on her own – all of it.

She looked at the little plants Walter had given her. They seemed to have grown since this morning; another pair of tiny pointed leaves sprouting from the tip of each plant. She looked at the packet lying on the window-sill. *Cosmos*. She could hear Walter's voice saying the word. 'My missus's favourite,' he had said. It was funny, the way she could sometimes remember what a word said. Out of curiosity, she looked at the next few words, expecting them to blur into meaningless squiggles, as they always did. *H . . . something . . . 3–5 feet*. That word must be *height*! She was sure of it. *Sow seeds in pots or trays . . .* She stopped. Her heart was pounding. She *knew* what the words meant. She had *read* them.

She hardly dared to look back at the packet, but she did. As she read the first words again, she realized that she was trembling. What if I can't do it? she thought. What if it was just an accident?

It had happened before like that, a long time ago when she was about six. She had chosen a reading book she wasn't supposed to have – a book about a magic door into another world. Her best friend Hayley had it for *her* reading book. Hayley could read really difficult books, and she had read it to Kate, over and over, showing off, until Kate could remember every word. So Kate had gone and chosen the same book for herself. Then she had waited her turn to read to the teacher. The memory came back vividly. The teacher had stopped her just as the best bit was beginning.

'Good, Kate,' she had said. 'Now let's go back. What was *that* word? There.'

The teacher had pointed with a red pen. Kate could still picture the sharp end, like a red claw, hovering over a word. The word had swum in front of her eyes and the meaning had slipped away in a sea of panic. The teacher had sighed and made a note on a pad.

'I don't really think you are ready for this yet, Kate. You should be reading . . . let's see . . . blue books. Level two. Off you go and find one you haven't read.'

Even now, years later, Kate felt the anger rising in her. She had taken the book, thrown it on the floor, and stamped on it. Then she had sat at her table with her head in her hands and refused to speak to anyone until Mum had arrived . . .

Kate shook herself. She looked again at the words on the packet. It wasn't easy. She wrestled with the words and letters, determined suddenly to find out what they meant.

Some words she wasn't quite sure about, but it all made sense. *Sow the seeds in pots or trays in a . . . greenhouse or on a warm . . . window-sill. Use a good . . . qu . . . qu . . . ality . . . compost. Sow thinly and cover the seeds with 6mm of . . . sieved compost . . .*

'What are you doing, Katie,' asked Emily. She was standing in the doorway with her bit of sheet, looking at Kate. 'Why were you crying?

'I wasn't,' Kate said. 'I was looking at my plants. Come and see.'

'You *have* been crying. There are wet bits on your face. I'll give you a hug if you like.' Emily put her arms around Kate, and now Kate couldn't stop the tears, but she was smiling at the same time. If she could learn to read properly, then school wouldn't be a problem. And if school wasn't a problem, then Mum and Dad wouldn't have to argue about it, and if they didn't have to argue . . . ?

'I like your little flowers,' said Emily. 'When are you going to plant them in the garden? We planted some at Nursery yesterday.'

'Soon,' said Kate. 'We're going to make a garden for Mum.'

The following day, Kate managed to take some books from Mike's room. She knew he'd never notice, not with the mess in there. She grabbed an encyclopaedia and a book about animals, and began to practise seriously. She didn't want anyone to know she could do it until she could do it properly. She felt the same way she had felt when she had first learned to ride a bike, not quite believing that she was really doing it, full of the fear that she was about to fall off.

Reading was hard work, but that didn't stop her. She forced herself to read on, hour after hour, and she finally fell asleep with a book in her hand. The next evening, she went up to her room as soon as she could, and carried on. Dad was busy on the computer downstairs, and she could hear the sound of a football commentary coming from the radio in Mike's room. Then she heard another sound, very quiet. She put down her book and went out onto the landing. The noise was coming from Emily's room. Kate opened the door and went in. Emily was snuffling quietly in her bed.

'What's the matter, Em?' Kate asked, sitting down on the edge of the bed.

'I want a story,' said Emily.

'But Dad read you one, didn't he?'

'Not like Mum does.'

'I'll tell you what,' Kate said, trying to keep her voice steady, 'I'll read you one. Which one would you like?'

'*Are You My Mother?*' said Emily at once. Kate knew the story. It had been her own favourite when she was little. The book was very battered, and the cover was falling off. Kate began to read. It was the first time in her life that she had ever read a whole book properly out loud to anyone. When she had finished, Emily was asleep, and Kate sat watching her for a long time, before she stood up and went downstairs. Dad was making cocoa.

'What have you been doing up there?' he asked. 'I've hardly seen you since Sunday.'

'Nothing,' Kate said.

Dad looked at her. He was quiet and serious, but that was a relief after the way he had been all these weeks. 'Fine,' he said. 'You keep it secret. At least you're looking a bit more cheerful.'

On Thursday night Kate and Mike arrived home to find Dad sitting at the kitchen table with Marty, the plumber. Marty was feeding Emily with bits of toasted crumpet. The kitchen was tidy for the first time since they had moved in.

'We're making plans,' said Dad through a mouthful of crumpet. 'Marty's going to help. He's going to plaster in here for a start.'

110

'I thought you were going to do it yourself,' Kate said. She felt oddly disappointed. 'I thought we were broke. And I thought *you* were a plumber,' she said to Marty, 'not a plasterer.'

'I do a bit of everything,' said Marty. 'Even babysitting.'

'More,' said Emily, tugging at the ring in Marty's lip with buttery fingers. Marty grinned and stuffed another bit of crumpet into her mouth.

'I had a stroke of luck today,' Dad said. 'My first big job as an independent consultant. So I can pay Marty with my own money. He's not taking over, mind. He's going to be my labourer. I'm in charge.'

Marty winked at Kate and raised one eyebrow.

'What was this job then?' asked Mike. 'It must have been good.'

'I saved a big company from a deadly computer virus,' said Dad. 'Lucky they rang me. Another ten minutes and their whole system would have been wiped out. I saved them a fortune, so they were very grateful. And now the word will really start to get around. Everything's going to work out. I can feel it in my bones.'

'You sound like Walter,' said Kate.

111

Dad laughed. 'It's probably soaking into me out of the timbers of the house,' he said. He widened his eyes and waved his fingers creepily towards Emily. She squeaked and grabbed Marty's hair. Like the old Dad, Kate thought. Then Dad asked, 'How is the old boy?'

'I don't know,' said Kate gloomily. 'I haven't seen him since the weekend. I think Louise's mum must have locked him in. The weeds are growing like mad in his garden. And I think Louise is avoiding me.'

"Billhook"

Chapter 10

It wasn't until lunch-time on Friday that Kate finally managed to talk to Louise.

'You can't keep this up for ever,' she said. 'Why weren't you on the bus?'

'Mum's been bringing me. Mr Grahame told her you were a bad influence. I'm not even allowed on the same bus as you.'

'You don't have to avoid me *here* though, do you?'

'I didn't think you'd want to talk to me. Not after the things Mum said to you.'

'Well, I do, OK? How's Walter?'

'He's under surveillance. That's what he calls it anyway. Mum pops in six or seven times a day to make sure he's all right. And she makes Dad go too. Grandad moans about them doing it, and they moan about having to do it. It's a nightmare.'

'Yes, but how *is* he?' asked Kate.

'It's hard to tell,' said Louise. 'The more Mum and Dad go on at him, the more miserable he gets. They won't even let him go outside. He hates sitting indoors all day.'

'I'm not surprised. I bet he's thinking about all those weeds growing in the garden, and him doing nothing about it. I ought to go and help.'

'No way!'

'Whose side are you on? One minute you say he's miserable, and the next you're trying to stop me doing anything about it.'

'You'll make it worse. You don't know my mum. She gets upset, but I bet she didn't mean what she said to you. Just stay away from Grandad for a few days and everything will be back to normal.'

'Oh yeah? And what about you? You said you'd help me. You promised.'

'I know.'

Kate waited a moment longer, then she turned and walked away. She looked back and saw Louise still standing there. 'I'm starting on Saturday,' she said. 'The garden. Come if you want.'

'I . . . I don't know,' said Louise. 'I'll try.'

Very early on Saturday morning, before anyone else was up, Kate went out into the garden, ready to begin. The nettles were growing incredibly fast. Already the lumps and bumps that had looked so promising were disappearing under waves of green. There was no time to waste. Kate made her way to the broken-down building where Dad kept the gardening tools. She fetched them out and lined them up against the wall. There was a small spade, a fork with bent prongs, a pair of shears and a lawnmower with blades that were rusted solid.

Dad had never been much of a gardener. There had been a small square of grass that belonged to their flat in London. Mum had persuaded Dad to make her a flowerbed once, but the army of wild cats that stalked the neighbourhood had dug up everything Mum had planted. The weeds had taken over. Dad had started calling the garden a Conservation Area. Mum hadn't laughed at the joke.

Kate picked up the shears and tried them on the undergrowth. The rusty blades seized a lump of grass and jammed themselves immovably together. She heard the back door open behind her, and Mike came out. 'It's weird, isn't it?' he said.

'What is?' Kate stood up, holding the shears in one hand.

'You know. It's Saturday, and Mum's not here.' Mike looked pale and tired, as if he hadn't slept properly. 'What are you doing, anyway?' he asked.

'I'm starting on the garden. Only, these tools are useless.'

'It's a jungle. You're wasting your time.'

'You'll just have to help then, won't you? You know Mum wants a garden. If we make her one . . .' Kate stopped. She had been going to say, 'If we make her a garden then she'll stay.'

'I'm not a baby, you know,' said Mike angrily. 'You think just because I'm not as old as you I don't know what's going on. Well I do. It's not just this weekend, is it? You think Mum and Dad might split up.'

Kate stared at him.

'It's true, isn't it? That's what you think.'

'No,' said Kate. But Mike just looked at her until she shook her head and looked away.

'Me too,' said Mike. They stood for a moment in silence.

'So, you're going to help with the garden, then?' Kate asked finally. It was a relief,

116

knowing that Mike knew. But Mike was still angry. Upset.

'Come off it,' he said. 'What difference is a *garden* going to make? Mum and Dad fight all the *time*. They don't even like each other. How's a garden going to change that?'

'That's not true. It's just everything going wrong that's made them like that. The house, and everything being such a mess.'

'And *you*,' said Mike quietly. 'Being in trouble all the time. Mum and Dad argue about that more than they argue about anything. You know they do. And we wouldn't have had to move here at all if it hadn't been for you.'

Mike turned and went inside. Kate stared after him. He couldn't have chosen any words which would have hurt her more. She walked blindly away from the house, thoughts and feelings spinning round inside her. How long had Mike been thinking those things? Why hadn't she realized? She'd thought Mike was OK; happy living inside his books, always ready with a joke. But he wasn't at all. He was just as upset as she was, or Emily. And he blamed *her*.

A bird began to sing loudly above her head, and the sun shone out from between the clouds. There was an answering gleam at Kate's feet. She looked down and saw a pale blue flower, only just opened. She sank to her knees and brushed some dead leaves aside. Everywhere, green spears were thrusting up through the matted grass. There were dozens of them, clustered around the mossy trunk of an old tree, each covered in buds about to burst. She began to search in widening circles, pulling at the grass, hardly daring to put her feet or hands down in case she broke a shoot. She was concentrating so hard that she didn't hear Louise arrive, pushing a creaking wheelbarrow. Then Louise yelled in pain as a bramble caught her leg, and Kate looked up and saw her. She stood up, and stretched her aching back. Just being in the garden, doing something, had made her feel a million times better. It wasn't as if Mike had said anything she hadn't thought herself. What mattered now was the garden. 'Look what I've found,' she called to Louise. 'Do you know what they are?'

'Bluebells!' exclaimed Louise. 'I remember. When I was little. When they're all out they look like the sea. There must be all kinds of things hidden under all this.'

'I didn't think you'd come,' Kate said.

'Mum and Dad have gone out. They're looking for homes for Grandad again. They left me at Grandad's house. We're supposed to be

118

looking after each other, but he said I ought to come and help you. He gave me this. Look.'

She was holding a dog-eared black book. Kate took it, and opened it. The pages were yellow with age, and covered with faded brown writing and tiny, beautiful drawings. Drawings of flowers and leaves; drawings of benches and walls. Each page had a date at the top. 'It's Grandad's diary from when he was making the garden,' Louise told her. 'When I got there this morning he'd been up in the attic, looking for it. He could have broken his neck. Luckily, Mum didn't catch him. He made me bring this lot, too.'

The wheelbarrow was full of tools. Kate reached down and pulled out a pair of shears. The blades glinted brightly in the sun.

'I think he's been getting them ready specially,' Louise said.

Kate attacked a clump of grass with the shears. The blades hissed together and sliced through the tangled mess as if it wasn't there. 'Hey!' she said. 'These are brilliant!' She stood up with her eyes shining, and pulled another tool from the barrow. It looked like an outsized butcher's cleaver with a hooked end. Its edge was wickedly sharp. 'What's this?' she asked.

'That's a billhook,' said Walter's voice. 'You be careful with that or you'll have your arm

119

off.' Pups rushed past Walter, and jumped up at Kate before she could stop him, licking her on the nose.

'What are you *doing* here, Grandad?' Louise gasped, horrified. 'You *promised* you'd stay in and watch the racing. Mum will go crazy.'

'Not if you don't tell her, she won't. I'll be back in my kitchen by the time she come round with my tea, and she won't know no different. Now then, let's have a look.' Walter walked between the two girls and gazed at the over-grown garden.

Kate looked at Louise. 'What are you going to do?' she whispered.

'What *can* I do? Stop him doing too much, I suppose. And make sure he gets back home in plenty of time. This is what I was trying to tell you . . .'

Walter stopped. 'I en't deaf,' he snapped. 'I've had enough of people telling me what's good for me, that's all. So why don't you stop fussing and get started?'

Chapter 11

'Not like that!' said Walter. 'Give me the spade, girl.'

'No way!' said Kate, pulling the spade away from him. 'That's all we need – you injuring yourself. Just tell me what I'm doing wrong.'

Walter laughed. 'Everything!' he said.

'Oh, thanks. That's a big help.'

'Well, if you won't let me show you . . .'

Kate began hacking at the matted grass again. There was something hard underneath, but the spade wouldn't cut through the thick tangle of roots. She swore.

121

'Just you slow down a minute,' Walter said, 'or that'll be you that gets hurt. Push the spade in and find the edge of the path. That's over there somewhere, I reckon.' Walter pointed to the ground. Kate stabbed with the spade. It clinked on stone. 'Keep trying. Bit further over.' A soft thud this time. 'That's it. Now you put your foot on the spade and press right down. Go on. Hard!'

Kate brought all her weight down on the spade and suddenly she felt something give. The blade cut deep into the earth. Kate nearly fell flat on her face.

'Right,' said Walter with a grin, 'now you got a start. You keep going along here. Then you can get the spade underneath, see? Lift it off the stones.' Kate chopped down a couple more times and then pushed the spade in sideways, under the grass and roots. There was a grating sound.

'Yes!' exclaimed Kate. She levered upwards with the spade and revealed a patch of dark brown stone. Walter and Louise came closer to look.

'That's it!' said Walter. 'Laid that stone myself, I did. Forty year ago.' He was as excited as a little kid. Kate chopped harder at the grass, and finally managed to pull a big lump clear.

'There!' she said, out of breath. 'I've done it!'

'You've made a start,' Walter told her, 'but that's going to be a big old job. Look at it!'

Kate stood on the patch of path as Walter walked away from them, along the front of the house, trampling weeds and nettles as he went. 'The path end about here, I reckon,' he called, 'and there's a bit that go off down there.' He pointed at the densest thicket of brambles.

Dad appeared at the back door. He was in his pyjamas. 'Kate?' he said. 'What's going on?'

'I'm starting on the garden,' Kate told him. 'Louise and Walter have come to help.'

'So you're Louise,' said Dad. 'Nice to meet you at last. From what Kate told me I thought you were a prisoner. And is that your grandad? I thought he was ill.' Dad waved at Walter.

'It's OK, Dad.' Kate didn't give Louise a chance to answer. 'Walter's just telling us what to do. He's not doing any work.'

'But . . . it's a wilderness, Kate. Look at it. You'll never do anything with it. Not the two of you. It needs a digger. It needs half a dozen diggers and a chainsaw. You know I haven't got time to help you.'

'You don't understand,' said Kate. 'There's a garden here already. A real one. Look.'

Dad stared at the paving slab. 'That's a bit of stone,' he said. 'It's not a garden.'

'But it is,' Kate insisted.

'That's not as bad as it looks,' Walter added. He shook hands with Dad. 'If they'd just let me have a go with that spade . . .'

'You've done the plumbing,' Kate said. 'None of us thought you could . . .' Dad started to interrupt, but Kate carried on, '. . . so why can't we do the garden? And anyway, it's not *for* you. It's for Mum.'

There was a silence. Kate could see that Dad understood. He turned to Walter. 'It's very good of you to help them, Mr Fuller. Just make sure you don't let Kate take advantage of you. You don't know what she's like.'

'Dad! As if I would.'

'Yes, well. How about a cup of tea, Mr Fuller? I'll show you what I've been doing inside. We're going to start plastering later on . . .'

Dad led Walter firmly away.

The girls worked on. As the stones of the path emerged one by one, the work began to seem easier. Kate chopped out the strips of turf, then Louise lifted them and carried them to the side of the path. A pile began to grow beside them. As Louise turned with her latest spadeful, she saw that a robin had flown down and was

124

sitting on top of the heap, watching. She nudged Kate.

'Look at him. He's not even scared!'

'There's one in Walter's garden. D'you think it's the same one? Maybe it followed him here.'

Louise laughed. 'No way! Robins have territories. Not very big territories either. There are two in Grandad's garden, and you sometimes see them fighting. This is *your* robin. Keep very still. I bet he's looking for food.'

As Kate stood watching she felt the aches throbbing in her back and her arms and her legs. She was starting to ache all over. She was going to be very stiff. But it didn't matter. She was doing this for Mum.

The robin didn't move. Birds were singing everywhere. Something fluttered through the undergrowth. The garden was alive. Far away across the fields she heard the drone of a tractor. Louise shook her arm. The robin had flown closer. It looked nervously from side to side as it stabbed at the soil with its beak. Peck. Swallow. And then a sudden flight and the robin was sitting on the branch of a tall bush, watching again.

'You say you hate all this,' Kate said, 'but you don't, do you? Not really. You're at home here. You know all about birds – *and* cows. I bet you know what that tractor's doing over there. It's like a foreign country to me.'

'I don't know what I want,' said Louise. 'I want to *be* something, that's all. And I want Grandad to be well again. Really well.' She picked up a lump of grass and flung it onto the top of the heap. Kate bent her aching back to start work again.

A little later, Dad appeared with a tray. 'Elevenses,' he said. 'I'm kicking everyone outside now. I've got to clear the kitchen. I've brought Walter a chair so he can supervise you.'

Mike was holding the chair. He stared at the path, astonished. 'It's brilliant,' he exclaimed.

'I told you, didn't I?' said Kate. Dad had walked off along the back of the house with Walter.

'I didn't realize.' Mike brushed some earth from the stones. 'This all looks really old. There could be anything buried under here. Secret passages even.'

'I don't think so.'

'I'm sorry about earlier.' Mike hesitated. 'I didn't mean it. I was upset.'

'Yeah, well . . .' Kate felt embarrassed, but at the same time she felt as if a weight had been lifted from her. 'Does this mean you're going to help, then?'

'What do you want me to do?'

'You could get rid of that lot, for a start.' Kate pointed to the pile they had made.

As Dad disappeared inside, Walter came over to join them. He ignored the waiting chair. 'Over there,' he said, 'behind those bushes.' He seized a billhook from the wheelbarrow and moved off, slashing at the undergrowth.

They worked all morning, and for lunch Dad cooked spaghetti. Walter wolfed it down. He looked ten years younger. Marty arrived as they were clearing up.

'What you doing here, Uncle Walter?' he said. 'I thought Debs had you under control.'

'Uncle?' said Kate.

'Well, I call him that,' Marty grinned, 'but he might be some sort of cousin. I can never work it out. There's dozens of Fullers round here and I reckon we're all related somehow or other. You lot had best be out of here. I've got a vanload of plaster to bring in.'

Outside, Mike picked up a spade and started clearing more of the path. Walter began poking about in the undergrowth. Kate and Louise followed him. No matter how careful Kate was, she couldn't stop the nettles from stinging her.

Walter laughed. 'You'd better get used to that,' he said. 'You'll have worse than that to put up with before you're finished. Once your hands get like mine you won't even notice.' He grabbed a nettle and pulled it out of the ground. 'See. Don't hurt a bit.'

Kate looked at Louise and they both smiled. Kate had seen Walter wince as the nettle stung him. He acted tough, but he was as soft as anything inside. She looked at Walter's face. He was miles away. *The garden's still there*, she thought, *inside his head*. 'Walter?' she said gently, touching his arm. 'What are you thinking?'

For a moment Walter looked like a man waking from a deep sleep. Then he smiled. 'We'd better have a look, hadn't we? Down at the bottom there, that's where . . .' He stopped. He had seen the bluebells.

'I found them this morning,' said Kate. 'They're lovely. Did you plant them?'

Walter nodded. 'Let's see what else is left,' he said. 'We'll need a spade and a pair of shears I reckon.'

Kate ran back, ignoring the stings, and returned quickly with the tools. Walter had already trampled a clearing in the nettles, and was on his knees, probing carefully with his fingers.

'I knew it!' he said. 'That take a lot to kill these things. Look!' Walter took the shears from Kate and cleared a space where he had been searching. 'See that?' he said, pointing to a few pale, spindly stalks, 'Know what that is? That's a . . .'

'Delphinium,' said Louise.

Walter looked up. 'I never thought you'd remember,' he said. 'I thought the book learning would have driven it all out of your head.'

'I just knew,' said Louise. 'I looked at it, and the name was there. I know the weeds, too.' She pointed. 'That's bindweed. That's chickweed. And that . . .' She picked up a tiny creeping plant with dark leaves and a deep blue flower. 'That's ground ivy.'

'Well, I don't know,' said Walter. 'Maybe you don't need me after all.' He tugged at the weeds around the delphinium. 'Give this some light. Fork a bit of muck in around here. There's a few old heaps of it over where we dumped the weeds. That'll be flowering in a month or two.' He stood up and looked around. 'And there!' he said. 'Look at that.'

Kate looked where he was pointing. All she could see was a wall of brambles, but Walter took the shears and began cutting through them. Kate reached out to pull one of the long, trailing stems away from Walter's feet.

'Don't!' warned Walter, but it was too late. Kate pulled her hand away with a cry. The thorns were like razors. A drop of blood fell from her finger. 'You'll need a good pair of gloves,' Walter said. 'But see here.' From the tangle of thorns a slender branch had appeared, full of buds. '*Philadelphus*,' he told her. 'That smell lovely. All white, that is.'

'Weird names,' said Kate.

'Latin, see. You wouldn't think an old boy like me would know Latin, would you. They say that's a dead language.'

Walter led the girls on through the garden, pointing out plants. His excitement grew with each new discovery. To Kate's astonishment, Louise knew the names of almost all of them. Kate looked back. She could no longer see the house. The garden was even bigger than she had thought. They paused in front of the biggest clump of brambles of all. 'Here,' said Walter. 'This is where . . .'

Kate saw Marty struggling through the bushes towards them.

'Hey, Walter, what are you up to now?' he said. His hair was dusted with pink powder, and his blue overalls were covered with spots and smears of plaster. Kate saw a guilty expression pass briefly across Walter's face, and immediately she felt guilty herself. She glanced at Louise and saw she felt the same. They shouldn't have let him start. They should have been doing the hard work themselves.

'Come you out of there,' said Marty. 'Here, I'll give you a hand.'

'I was just taking a look,' Walter said.

'I didn't mean for him to start doing that,' Kate said. 'He just . . .'

'Not your fault,' Marty told her. 'Everyone know about Walter.' They walked slowly back the way they had come.

'I think I will just sit down for a minute,' Walter said. 'Where's that chair?'

Kate saw that Walter was leaning on Marty's arm. She saw that, beneath Walter's wrinkled brown skin, the blood had drained from his face. Walter let go of Marty's arm and reached for the back of the chair. He grabbed at it, and the chair slid away from him as he toppled to the ground and lay very still.

Barn Owl
eats field mice

owl pellet

Chapter 12

Walter lay on the ground, his head resting on a clump of grass. His lips were a horrible greyish blue. Louise and Mike were like statues. Marty hesitated, then pulled a phone from his pocket. He began to dial as Kate knelt beside Walter. She put a hand out to touch his forehead. It felt cold and damp. She didn't know what to do.

'Yes. Ambulance please.' Marty spoke quickly into the phone. And suddenly Dad was there. He moved Kate gently to one side, and began talking to Walter. Kate felt Emily's small hand push into hers. She squeezed it and stepped backwards.

'Walter!' said Dad, shaking him gently by the shoulder. 'Walter? Can you hear me? Are you OK?'

'He was looking at the garden,' Kate said. 'I shouldn't have let him. He was cutting things down. And then we came back here and he went pale and he just . . . fell over.'

Dad was bending low over Walter's face now. He tilted Walter's head back, opened his mouth and looked inside, then he put his lips over Walter's lips, held his nose, and breathed twice into his mouth. Kate gripped Louise's arm. Mike took Emily's hand and led her away, gently.

'Dad,' Kate asked, 'is he . . . ?'

But Dad was feeling urgently at Walter's neck. 'Thank God for that,' he said. 'There's a pulse. Not much of one, but it's there.' He breathed again into Walter's mouth, and again. And then, suddenly, Walter took a breath on his own. Kate saw the colour return slowly to his lips, but he didn't open his eyes. Dad lifted him and sat him against the wall.

'We need some blankets,' he said. 'Quick as you can.' Kate raced into the house and tore the duvet off her bed. Pups pushed his nose against Walter's hand, trying to lift it, trying to make Walter stroke him.

'Come on, boy,' said Marty, grabbing hold of the collar. 'I'd best put you inside.' Dad nodded as he placed the duvet over Walter and tucked it carefully around him.

'Louise,' said Dad, 'how can we get in touch with your mum and dad?'

'I . . . there's a mobile . . . I can never remember the number . . . I'm sorry.' Louise began to cry. Kate put an arm round her.

'It's OK,' she said. 'He's going to be all right. Isn't he, Dad?'

'Sure,' said Dad. But Kate could see from his face that he wasn't sure at all.

Ten minutes later the ambulance arrived. Two paramedics bundled Walter onto a stretcher while Dad explained to them what had happened. Marty followed the men into the back of the ambulance.

'OK,' said Dad, as they watched it disappear, 'into the car, everyone. We'll go to your house first, Louise. That number must be written down somewhere.' Louise nodded. 'Good. We'll let your mum and dad know what's happened, then we'll go to the hospital.'

Kate didn't remember much about the next four hours. When they reached the hospital, the Fullers' Range Rover was already in the car park. Louise ran to her dad and clung to him. Kate, Mike and Emily hung back as Dad went over to talk to Louise's mum and dad. After a few moments, Dad returned.

'I don't think there's any point us hanging around. Apparently he's going to have to stay in for tests. And we wouldn't be able to see him anyway.'

'But is he going to be all right?' asked Kate.

'They won't know that until they've done the tests. But he's in the best place.'

'Were they angry?'

'Angry?' Dad looked at Kate's worried face. 'Oh, I see. About him being at our house, you mean? No-one's blaming you, Kate. And you mustn't blame yourself, either.'

Kate didn't say anything. She couldn't believe that Mrs Fuller hadn't said something to Dad about Walter being at their house. She could still see him, slashing at the brambles. She should have stopped him . . .

'Hey!' yelled Marty, running from the hospital door. 'Wait for me!' He arrived, panting. 'Can you give me a lift? Debs and Ted won't be going back for hours.'

'How is he?' demanded Kate.

'Well, now,' said Marty, 'when I left they were trying to get him to put this hospital gown on. You should have heard him going on

135

at them! Wanted his own pyjamas, he did. I felt right sorry for the nurses.'

Kate began to laugh. She couldn't stop herself. And before she knew it, she was crying with relief. 'I thought . . . I thought he was going to die.'

'Not just yet,' said Marty. 'He's a tough old beggar.'

The light was fading from the sky when they arrived home. Everything was just as they had left it. It was only when they got out of the car that they heard Pups barking. When Dad opened the back door, Pups rushed outside and then stopped. He sniffed at each of them in turn, and then simply sat down, as if he didn't know what to do. Kate forgot her fear of dogs as she stroked his soft black head.

'I told Debs I'd take him home with me,' Marty said.

'Can't he stay here?' asked Kate.

'We haven't got any food for him,' said Dad. 'I don't think . . .'

'It's OK,' said Marty, looking at Kate. 'You keep him. I'll bring some food round in the morning.'

Kate looked gratefully at Marty. The others followed him round to the front of the house to say goodbye, but Kate stayed by the back door with Pups. In front of her was the path. Old flagstones, stretching along the back of the house, brushed clean. Mike had done it – finished it while she and Louise had been with Walter. And she hadn't even noticed. Inside, the phone began to ring. Kate ran to answer it. When she heard Mum's voice, she couldn't speak.

'Kate? Is that you? What's wrong?' Tears were rolling down Kate's cheeks. 'Kate? Tell me. What's the matter?'

'Mum, it's Walter. He's in hospital.'

'Walter? You mean the old man with the hat? Neighbourhood watch? That one? Well, he *is* an old man, love. Nothing to get upset about. How are things at school?'

'We were . . . He was . . .' Kate stopped. It was no good. She couldn't explain about Walter without explaining about the garden. And the garden *had* to be secret. So much had happened since Mum had left. Mum didn't understand any of it. Walter was just another old man to her.

'It's not more trouble at school, is it? I thought things were going well. Dad said . . .'

'That's all you ever think about. I don't care about school. I wouldn't care if it burned down tomorrow. Oh, what's the use . . .'

Kate smashed the phone down on the table.

Mum's voice was still squeaking from the receiver. Dad came into the room. He glanced from Kate to the phone, and then picked it up.

'Sarah? Well, of course she's upset. Anyone would be. Yeah, that's right, the old man with the dog. Dog's here in fact. Taken a bit of a shine to Kate. Yes. He'd come round to . . .' Kate seized Dad's arm and mouthed words at him. DON'T TELL HER ABOUT THE GARDEN. 'He'd come to . . . to look at the work we've done on the house . . .' Kate heard Mum's laughter. Then she must have asked a question, because Dad said, 'Well, because he's interested, of course . . . because he used to live here. I must have told you.' There was more squawking from the phone. 'Yes, well,' Dad said, 'you'll be astounded. I've . . .' Dad paused. 'No. I won't spoil the surprise. You can wait and see for yourself. When are you . . . ?'

There was a long silence. Then Dad said, 'Oh. But I thought . . .' Then Mum's voice again, talking. On and on.

A mask fell over Dad's face. Cold and miserable. The new, happy, confident Dad vanished behind it. After a few moments, Dad called for Mike and Emily to come to the phone. Kate didn't have to ask what Mum had said. It was obvious. *I can't come back yet. I need more time on my own.* Corny lines that Kate had heard a hundred times from the characters in *Beech Grove*. Suddenly, she felt as if they were *all* characters in a soap. But she couldn't bear to see Dad like this. She followed him into the computer room. He was sitting in his chair, staring at the blank screen.

'Dad? It's better this way. The more we can finish before Mum comes, the better. I don't *want* her to come. Not until the garden's finished.'

'Oh, Kate.' Dad turned to her, and smiled in spite of himself. 'You can't go on with the garden.'

'Of course I can. It's what Walter would want.'

Kate couldn't sleep that night. She lay in bed, watching moonlit clouds move slowly across the sky. There was another thing. A thing she had almost forgotten with everything that had happened. She could *read*, really read. She had been practising every day, and every night Emily had been getting two bedtime stories. One from Dad, and a second, secret one from her. She was slow, but getting faster all the time. And what was the first thing Mum always, *always* asked her about? School. A picture began to form in her mind. Mum opening the brown envelope that held her school report. Mum's jaw dropping as she read the words: *Kate has made excellent progress this term.*

Why not? Kate thought. I could do it if I wanted. She tried to imagine what it would be like, being with Mum without the black cloud of school always hovering over their heads. Another image filled her mind. Her and Mum working together in the garden, the way she had worked with Louise today. Smiling at each other and laughing. Why shouldn't it be like that?

She got out of bed and went to the window. The air outside was full of smells. The smell of earth. The smell of things growing and changing. She heard an owl screech, and saw the ghostly white shape floating silently along the hedgerow, brilliant in the moonlight. She yawned and climbed back into bed. She heard the owl call again, fading away into the distance. And then she was asleep.

The next thing she knew it was light and Pups was lying on the end of the bed. She didn't know how he had got there. Emily was sleeping beside her with her fingers in her mouth. This is getting ridiculous, she thought. She eased herself out of bed without disturbing Emily. Her whole body seemed to be aching from yesterday's work, but there was a job she had to do. She shook Mike awake. 'I'm going to Walter's,' she said, as he struggled to open his eyes.

She took the hoe from its place in the shed and began to work. It was far harder than it had been the last time. Pups lay on the path and watched her.

A carpet of small green plants covered the whole garden. It was hard to see which were vegetables and which were weeds. Louise would know, but she wasn't here. *It's no good thinking*, she told herself. *Just get on with it.* She put down the hoe and bent to pull the weeds out with her hands. She worked slowly along the row, and was so absorbed in the green world between her fingers that she didn't hear the gate opening.

'You!' said Mrs Fuller. 'What are you doing?'

Kate stood up. Mrs Fuller's face was drawn and tired. 'I'm only weeding,' she said. 'I'm not doing any harm.'

'No. You've done enough of that already, haven't you?'

Kate stood without saying anything. She didn't deserve this. She was trying to help. I won't cry, Kate told herself. I won't. But Mrs Fuller's accusation pierced her. She put a muddy hand to her face.

141

'Oh, Kate. I'm sorry. I didn't mean . . .' Mrs Fuller hurried up the path. 'Look, it's been a nightmare for all of us since Louise's grandma died. And I *was* angry when Louise got into trouble. She'd been doing so well. But you mustn't think we blame you for what happened yesterday.'

'But . . .'

'I know I said you shouldn't encourage him. But this could have happened any time. In a way it's lucky it happened when it did. If your dad hadn't been there . . .'

'I only wanted to keep his garden tidy. It's such a mess. He'll worry about it.'

'You don't have to. There really isn't any need.'

'But I want to. I want to help.'

Pups nuzzled at her hand. Then he nuzzled at Mrs Fuller's hand. 'It was a help, you looking after Pups,' Mrs Fuller said. 'I don't know what I'm going to do with him. Kennels, I suppose.'

'You can't!' said Kate. 'He could stay with us. I'm sure Dad wouldn't mind.'

Mrs Fuller smiled. 'He seems to like you,' she said. 'I'll talk to your dad later.'

'Did you hear that?' Kate said to Pups. 'You're coming to stay with us.'

'But all this weeding,' Mrs Fuller continued.

'It's too much. I should think you've enough to do with your own garden. It was more than I could ever manage. It's a lovely idea, doing that for your mum.'

Kate stared at Mrs Fuller. What had Louise told her? How *could* she?

'Go and see Walter in hospital,' Mrs Fuller said. 'You can go this afternoon. He'd love to see you. I'll ring your dad and tell him – and we can talk about Pups. Now, I'd better go and find Walter some pyjamas.'

Kate watched Mrs Fuller walk up the path. Then she looked at the garden. *I can't*, she thought. *I can't just leave it*. She picked up the hoe and began to chop savagely at the weeds.

Chapter 13

'The food's terrible,' said Walter. He was sitting up in bed wearing a white hospital gown. 'And I want my own pyjamas. This thing don't do up properly. I thought Debbie was bringing them.'

'She collected them this morning,' said Kate.

'Well, where are they, then?'

'She was at your house when I was doing the weeding. She looked tired. I expect she'll be here later. And Walter, Pups is staying at our house. He misses you, but we're looking after him.'

Walter didn't seem to hear what Kate said. 'They keep pulling me about,' he grumbled, 'Sticking needles into me. I tell them there's nothing wrong with me. I come over a bit dizzy, that's all that was. And what you brought them primulas for?' Emily was clutching a small pot of flowers. She had chosen them herself. She looked as if she was going to cry.

'They'll die in here,' Walter went on. 'That's like an oven. I keep telling them to open a window. Let some air in. I want to go home.'

'He's giving them nonstop bother,' said a red-faced man in the next bed. 'I reckon they'd send him home today if they could. You got to listen to them doctors, mate,' he said to Walter.

'I en't your mate,' said Walter.

'See what I mean,' said the man.

Kate tried telling Walter about the garden. 'You won't believe how much we've done. Mike especially. You can see the whole path. You can see where the terrace begins.' Walter grunted. He hardly seemed to hear. Kate glanced at Mike and Dad. They were both shifting uncomfortably on the hard chairs. 'I went round and marked all the plants you showed us. And I'm going to do what you said. I'll clear all the weeds away and put muck around them. Then I'm going to start on the lawn . . .'

Kate kept talking. She felt she had to.

Whenever she stopped, the silence was terrible. She was glad when a smiling nurse appeared.

'I'm afraid you'll have to leave now,' she said. 'We've to do a few more tests on Mr Fuller.'

'See what I mean?' said Walter. 'They won't let me alone.'

'Oh, come on, Walter,' said Kate. 'Stop grumbling. They're only trying to make you better.'

'I en't ill.'

'Yes, you are. You know you are. But you'll get better. You've got to get better to help us with the garden.'

Kate looked into Walter's eyes and knew that he was scared. All his grumbling and bad temper was just to cover up. They looked at each other for a moment, then Walter turned to the nurse. 'Well?' he said. 'What are you waiting for?' He turned back to Kate, Emily and Mike. 'Thanks for bringing the flowers,' he said. 'Thanks for looking after the old dog. And thanks for coming to see me.' He ruffled Emily's curly hair. 'You'll come again?'

Kate nodded. She reached out and held Walter's hand as the nurse began pulling curtains round his bed.

As they were leaving, they met the Fullers. Kate couldn't look at Louise. She walked straight past her. Louise ran after her down the corridor.

'Kate? What is it?'

'You told your mum.'

'I don't understand. Told her what?'

'You told her about *my* mum. About the garden.'

'I didn't. I don't know what I said. I thought Grandad was going to die. I only said you were doing it for your mum. I never said . . . I never said she . . . I wouldn't.'

And now Kate noticed Louise's face. She looked as if she had been crying for hours. 'I'm sorry,' Kate whispered. 'I should have known.'

'Mum said you were weeding his garden.' Kate nodded. 'I'll help, OK?'

'Are you sure?' Kate said.

'Of course I'm sure. Tomorrow. After school.'

By the time they got home Kate was so stiff that she knew she couldn't do any more gardening today. Pups seemed to be tired, too. He flopped down on her bed and went to sleep. If she was going to do some homework she'd have to start now. She emptied the school bag onto her table. Her geography book was on top. She could hear Mr Grahame's voice telling them what to do.

'*Go away and think, if that's possible, about*

147

the way our transport system should be organized in the future. Consider all the issues we've discussed. Then write me a newspaper article about it. OK?'

He hadn't been talking to *her*, of course. Like every other teacher, he had learned that it was easiest to leave Kate alone. Kate had watched loads of TV programmes about pollution and road-building. She loved the people who dug tunnels and built tree-houses to try to stop them building roads. She could *definitely* write about that. She started to write. Only, writing wasn't the same as reading. She wrote the words, but they just didn't look right. And she didn't know why. She didn't hear Mike come into the room.

'Kate? What are you doing?'

'Get out. Who said you could come in here?' Kate scrunched the paper into a ball.

'The door was open. You were writing something. You never . . .'

'I told you. Go away.' Kate was nearly crying. Mike turned, then stopped and said, 'I could help you.'

'Oh, yeah? Just leave me alone.'

Kate threw the ball of paper at the bin. It missed and rolled across the floor. Mike picked it up.

'Hey! Give me that.' Kate crossed the room and tried to grab the paper.

She was too late. Mike was already reading what she had written.

'OK,' she said. 'Go on, then. Laugh.'

Mike ignored her. He carried on studying what she had written. 'You know what?' he said at last. 'A spell check would sort most of these out for you.'

'What do you mean?'

'You must have used a word processor. Everyone does.'

'Not me.' In Kate's mind, computers were for playing games, and if she couldn't do that, she wasn't interested.

'I'll show you. Dad's not using the computer. He's too busy painting.'

In Dad's room, Mike started the program. 'You just type, see? And if you make a mistake, the computer tells you. Look.' Mike typed *hapy* and the computer underlined it in red. 'Click here, see? Can you see what it should be?'

Kate looked at the list on the screen. *Happy* was right at the top. As soon as she saw it, she knew it was right.

'Hey!' said Kate. 'That's dead simple. Why didn't you show me before?'

'Are you kidding? Remember when I started at the Infants school, and I learned to read? And then I started trying to help you with your book. You remember what you did?'

Kate flushed. It wasn't a happy memory. She had nearly wrecked Mike's bedroom. Mum and Dad had had to separate them. 'Yeah, well,' she said, 'what do you think it feels like when your baby brother can read better than you? They all made such a fuss of you. I felt about two centimetres high.'

They looked at each other for an uneasy moment, then Mike said, 'I never thought. But you must see what I mean. It's about as easy to show you how to do something as it is to get Walter to slow down – or to get Dad to do one of the things on Mum's lists.'

'You . . .' Kate stopped herself. She couldn't really argue. It was true. And anyway, she had things to do. She began to type, very slowly, with one finger.

'What's this?'

Mr Grahame had taken the work from Kate's hand, and then realized who she was.

'It's my homework, sir.'

'I didn't set *you* any homework.'

'No. But I wanted to do it. It was interesting.'

'Oh, so it's you who decides what you want to do now, is it?'

One or two kids were beginning to laugh. This was obviously another of Kate's windups. She'd been very quiet lately. Maybe things were going to liven up.

'I just thought . . .'

'Thinking now, as well, are we? Well, that's certainly a change for the better. Let's have a look.' Mr Grahame inspected Kate's work. After a few moments he looked up. 'I thought as much. Copied directly from a book. Or from a newspaper. Not even in your own hand-writing. I don't suppose you have a clue what it means. Here, take it. Don't waste my time like this again.'

Kate stared at him. This was something she hadn't expected. She could feel the anger building inside her. 'I spent *hours* doing that. I didn't copy a *word* of it. I did just what you said. I've written what I think.'

'Now you're being ridiculous. You've never written me more than a sentence before, and now you expect me to . . . Stop that! What do you think you're doing?'

Kate opened her exercise book and ripped it in half from top to bottom. Blood pounded in her ears. There was a stunned silence in the class-room. Everyone stared at Mr Grahame. But Kate hadn't finished. She threw the pieces of the book on the floor, and then she emptied her bag onto the desk next to her. One by one, she picked up the books and tore them in half, adding them to the pile on the floor. Finally, she peeled off the orange sweatshirt and threw it at Mr Grahame. He caught it without thinking.

'That's what I think of your stupid school. You can keep it. I'm going home.' Kate started to move. And now, finally, Mr Grahame acted. He moved quickly to put himself between Kate and the door.

'Carl, fetch Mrs Denby. Go on, boy! Do it now.'

Kate watched the emotions running across Mr Grahame's face. He was angry, but he was worried too. Kate didn't move. She knew there wouldn't be long to wait. The silence stretched on. Then the door opened and Mrs Denby came in.

'At last,' said Mr Grahame. 'I have never witnessed behaviour like this in my entire career. I trust . . .'

Mrs Denby held up a hand. 'I don't want to discuss this now,' she said. 'Kate, go to my office. Mr Grahame, you may join us when you have finished teaching.'

'I'm going home,' said Kate.

'I dare say,' said Mrs Denby grimly.

Nobody laughed. Kate's heart was still beating fast as she picked up her empty bag and followed the headteacher out of the room.

Chapter 14

Before they reached the end of the corridor Kate heard running footsteps behind her. It was Louise. She was clutching the two halves of Kate's geography book in her hand. 'Mrs Denby,' she panted, 'it wasn't Kate's fault.'

'No?' Mrs Denby raised her eyebrows.

'Don't waste your breath,' said Kate. 'She's going to throw me out anyway. I don't know why I even bothered to try. It would have happened sooner or later, whatever I did.'

'Just take this,' said Louise. 'It's what Kate wrote.' She thrust the pieces of the book at

Mrs Denby, then turned and walked away.

'Extraordinary!' said Mrs Denby. 'I don't know what's got into that girl. Come along, Kate. We've called your father and he is on his way.'

Mrs Denby sat behind her desk. Kate watched as she took a pair of spectacles from a drawer, placed the pieces of the book carefully together, and began to read. Kate knew it wouldn't make any difference. Now that her anger had gone she felt sick. It was so unfair. She had only been trying to make things better. It seemed as if everything she touched fell to pieces. Walter was in hospital, and now she was about to get thrown out of another school. What was Mum going to say . . . ?

'Mr Oakley,' the secretary announced, and Dad came into the room. Kate nearly laughed. He looked exactly as if he was the one who had done something wrong. He glanced at Kate and then shook hands with Mrs Denby.

'I'm sorry to drag you in like this, Mr Oakley,' Mrs Denby said, 'but there has been a very serious incident. Perhaps you'd like to tell your father your version of events, Kate?'

'What's the point? No-one wants me here. I don't learn anything. And when I do try and do something, the teachers just laugh at me.'

'Calm down, Kate,' said Dad. 'Just tell me what happened, OK?'

'I did some homework, that's all. And he didn't believe I did it. He said I copied it. So I ripped my books up. That's it. Can we go now?'

'The thing is,' said Mrs Denby, 'this piece of work is very good. Fresh . . . interesting. But I still don't understand how you did it. All your teachers have told me that you've made no progress at all since you arrived here. I quite see why Mr Grahame would have found it hard to believe that you did this yourself.'

'But he was rude,' Kate burst out. 'He didn't even give me a chance. He made fun of me.'

'Can I see?' asked Dad. Mrs Denby handed him the book. 'You wrote this?' he said. 'But it's great. Fantastic. This bloke must be mad. Is he the one who rang me? The pompous idiot?'

'Really, Mr Oakley,' said Mrs Denby. 'I can't allow you to talk about one of my staff like that. It's not helpful.'

Kate saw a glint in Dad's eye. He sat up a little straighter in his chair. 'So what are you going to do then?' he asked.

'First of all, I'd like to see how you managed this, Kate. You did it on a computer. Can you show me?'

Kate was on her feet. 'You don't believe me either,' she shouted.

Dad touched her arm. There was a look on his face now that Kate hadn't seen before.

155

When he spoke, his voice was very calm and even. 'Just show her,' he said. 'Then they'll all have to believe you.'

'I shouldn't have to,' said Kate. 'Nobody trusts me.' She crossed the room to Mrs Denby's computer. She started up the word processor. It was the same as Dad's. She typed a few words, very slowly, then a wiggly red line appeared beneath one of them. Kate looked down the list and found the correct spelling. Then she carried on typing. Mrs Denby picked up Kate's book. 'But this must have taken you *hours*,' she said.

'I'll get quicker,' Kate told her. Outside, morning break had begun. There was a knock on the door. The secretary came in and said that Mr Grahame was waiting.

'Tell him I'll see him this afternoon,' said Mrs Denby. Then she turned to Kate. 'I can't help you to keep your temper,' she said. 'You have to do that for yourself. And if you don't, then I'm afraid you can't stay in this school. We won't take this any further for now, on two conditions. You must apologize to Mr Grahame, and you must replace the books which you have ruined.'

'Now just hold on a minute,' said Dad. 'It seems to me this Mr Grahame has some apologizing to do as well.'

'I've already told you,' said Mrs Denby. 'I don't wish to discuss Mr Grahame.'

'Then we'd better go, hadn't we?' said Dad. He stood up. 'Kate? What are you waiting for?'

Mrs Denby got to her feet, but she didn't try to stop them. Kate felt as if she was dreaming. They walked straight out of the school gates, and got into the car. Dad sat in the driver's seat and Kate saw that his hands were shaking. 'What have I done?' he said.

'I don't know. What's going to happen?'

'Right now, we're going home,' Dad said. 'I'm not angry with you, Kate. And I think I know what I'm going to do. What *we're* going to do. But I need to think before I decide.'

Dad drove home without saying another word. When the car stopped, Kate opened the door.

'Wait,' said Dad. Kate closed the door again. 'It's true then?' Dad asked. 'You taught yourself to read?' Kate nodded. 'But why didn't you say?'

'I wanted to get good. And I have.'

'So how did you do it?'

'I don't know. I suppose the first thing was in the graveyard . . .' Dad stared at her. 'No, really . . .'

Kate told Dad the whole story. Somehow,

learning to read was all tied up with Walter, and the garden, and living here. 'What about all that stuff you do at school, then?' asked Dad, 'With that teacher. Mrs Cartwright? That must have helped.'

'I've been doing that stuff for *years*, Dad. I never learned to read before, did I? When I go into that place I feel sick. I can't do anything. It's always been like that.'

They got out of the car and went into the garden. 'If you didn't go to school,' said Dad, 'if I taught you at home. How would you feel about that?'

Kate stared at him. 'But how could you?'

'It can't be any harder than plumbing.'

Kate felt dizzy. She couldn't believe what Dad was saying. 'But Mum . . .'

'We've talked about it before,' Dad said. 'You've never exactly got on with schools, have you?'

'But Mum would never . . .'

'Well, no, she never agreed before. But this is different. We could do it. I know we could. Look at what you've done for yourself already. Look at all this. No-one can say you don't work hard. And anyway . . . Mum's not here, is she?'

'Don't be stupid, Dad. You'll . . . we'll have to tell her.'

158

'Yeah, but not just yet. We can tell her you're getting on well with your reading. By the time we see her you can have something really good to show her. How about a book about this garden? Like a diary. Everything you do.'

'Like Walter's,' said Kate. 'Like his old black book.'

'Exactly,' said Dad. 'You'd better get started, hadn't you?'

Inside the house, the phone was ringing. Dad picked it up. *'Mrs Denby . . . Yeah, well I'm sorry too . . .'* There was a long pause. Dad listened. *'Oh . . . Right . . . No, you're right, I wasn't expecting that . . . Well fine, thanks . . . Yes, I'll think about it. Goodbye.'* He put the phone down. 'Well, who would have thought it? he said.

'What? What's happened?'

'She says that teacher "went too far". She says he's going to apologize to you. She wants to know when you'll be back at school.'

Kate felt as if she had been given a present and it had suddenly been snatched away again. 'I don't care if he does apologize,' she said. 'What does it matter? He's the worst, but what about the rest. They just want me to keep quiet and not bother them.'

'You don't want to go back then?'

Kate stared at Dad. He was smiling. 'You mean . . . ?'

'I think we should give it a try.'

When Mike arrived home, Kate was in the garden digging a new patch of flowerbed. Emily was busy making mud pies and Pups was sniffing at each new spadeful of earth that Kate turned over. 'Dad told me,' Mike said.

'Well?' Kate stood up and leaned on her spade.

'I think it's brilliant.'

'You don't want to stay at home too?' Kate had been worrying about this all day.

Mike laughed. 'No way!' he said. 'No football, no basketball, no playtimes. I'd rather be with my mates. That's what I wanted to tell you. My mates. They all want to help.'

'What do you mean?'

'With the garden, stupid.' Kate thought of Mike's mates. They all looked like clones, hair neatly gelled at the front. Obsessed with football. She couldn't imagine them here, in the garden. Mike had no right.

'Why did you tell them?'

'You didn't say not to. They think it's cool, just like the TV.'

'You should have asked me,' Kate said angrily.

'Oh, come on,' said Mike. 'The garden doesn't *belong* to you, you know. And anyway, you should be grateful. You'll never finish it on your own. Not in a million years.'

Kate looked at the patches of flowerbed she had cleared. The walls were still hidden, and the lawn was a joke. They didn't even have a proper lawnmower. But even so . . . 'They won't do it properly,' she said. 'They'll start things and then they'll get bored and go off and play football.'

'No, they won't,' grinned Mike. 'I'll tell them, shall I? What have you got to lose? You'll still be in charge. We'll do what you say, honest.'

Chapter 15

Louise and Kate worked every evening, weeding Walter's garden. It took them a week to finish it. 'There's just one problem,' Kate said, as they looked at what they'd done. 'Have you seen the parsnips – where we started?'

They walked down the path and looked. Already, weeds were poking their heads above the surface. Louise sighed. 'It just goes on, doesn't it?' she said. 'We'll never be able to stop.'

'Not until Walter comes home,' said Kate.

'Even if he does come home he won't be able

to do all this, will he? You saw him yesterday.'

Kate and her family had been to the hospital the evening before. Louise had been this evening. Kate had been frightened by the change in Walter. He seemed to have shrunk. A little old man in a big hospital bed. He had been pleased to see them, but when Kate had tried to talk to him about her plans for the garden, he had grown very quiet. After a while he had fallen asleep.

'He's just tired,' said Kate. 'It's been a shock. He'll soon be feeling better. He's tough. You know he is.' She stopped when she saw that Louise was crying.

'He's going to die,' said Louise.

'He's not.'

'He's eighty-three. His heart's packing up.'

'So – what? Are you saying we should stop weeding his garden? We *can't* give up. What if he starts feeling better and he asks about it? When we tell him how we've been looking after it, it'll make him want to get home even more.'

'You're not *listening*, are you? I don't see how he *can* come home. He's too old and too ill. When he comes out of hospital, he'll go into a home. Mum's right. She was right all along.'

Kate picked up the hoe and began to work. Louise turned and headed for the gate. When she got there, she stopped and looked back at

163

Kate. Kate didn't look up, but there was a streak of mud on her face where she had wiped away her tears. Louise walked back up the path. She stood looking at the plants.

'I suppose it would be a bit of a waste,' she said. 'We might as well look after them until they've finished growing.'

'He's going to come home,' said Kate.

On the first morning of the Easter school holidays, Kate was woken by the sound of voices in the garden below her window.

'Yeah! To me!'

'No. Over here. On me 'ead.'

Kate groaned and pulled her pillow over her head. Mike's mates had arrived, and they were playing *football*. She looked at the time. It was 7.30. They were crazy. Then there was a knock on her door and Mike shouted, 'They're here!'

'Tell them to go away again.'

'Come on, Kate. There's loads to do.'

Then Emily jumped on the bed, and Kate knew there was no chance of any more sleep.

'This is it then,' said Dad when Kate reached the kitchen. 'The great garden makeover. They could make a TV programme about us. Me doing the house and you doing the garden.' Several mysterious boxes had appeared in the kitchen during the night. 'Tiles,' said Dad.

'Tiles for the walls and tiles for the floor. The dream kitchen is nearly complete.'

'Who's doing the tiling?' asked Kate.

'Need you ask?' said Dad.

'Isn't Marty helping?'

'He can't make it today. He did offer to give me a hand tomorrow, but I reckon I can handle this, no worries. Don't look at me like that. I've got much better. Look.' Dad reached for the DIY manual and flipped open the catch. 'See. That's what practice can do for you. Go on. You get on with the gardening.'

The first job was to clear away all the rubbish. Kate knew she couldn't let the boys loose on the flowerbeds. She kept finding new things growing in the garden and she was sure that not all of them were weeds. She gave the boys rakes and shears, and told them to cut the grass.

'Can't we just use a lawnmower?' said Darren, snipping at a hunk of grass with his shears. 'This will take for ever.'

'Have you *seen* the mower?' asked Kate. 'Think of this as a football pitch. When you've cleared it, you can have a game, can't you?'

'It's nearly as *big* as a football pitch,' grumbled Sam.

Kate grabbed a pair of shears and began to

cut. Her arms were strong from all the hoeing, and her hands were tough. She worked fast, and in no time she had cleared a flat space big enough for them all to stand in.

'Hey!' said Louise. 'I thought the boys were going to do that.'

'I was just showing them how,' Kate explained. 'Here you are, Sam.' She handed him the shears. 'Not a problem, is it?'

'Course not,' said Sam, trying to look cool. Kate and Louise walked away and left them to it.

'OK,' said Mike. 'Let's do it.'

'It's so big,' said Louise. 'It looks bigger every time I see it.' They watched Emily starting to dig in a small patch of bare earth.

'That's her bit of garden,' Kate said. 'She spends hours there. She digs for worms and she plants things. Then she digs them up again and makes mud pies. Actually the garden's about 60 metres long and 40 metres wide, including all the flowerbeds. Look, here's the plan.'

Kate held out the book that Dad had given her. The plan was beautifully drawn and coloured. Louise leafed through the pages. Each one was covered with drawings and neat, tiny writing. Some of Kate's spellings were a little strange – she couldn't always be bothered to go and check things on the computer, and half the time Dad was busy using it. But she spent hours each day on the book. She wanted it to be as much like Walter's as possible.

'This is fantastic!' exclaimed Louise, turning back to the plan. 'It looks like the ones they use in the TV programmes. It looks real.'

'Of course it's real. This is what we're going to do today, see?' Kate flipped the pages over. 'Next week we'll . . .'

'It's great!' said Louise. 'It must have taken ages. And your mum'll be amazed at what your dad's done. I looked in on the way through. The tiles are going to be brilliant.'

'Maybe. Come on, let's get started.'

'Hang on.' Louise laid a finger on the plan. 'This bit here. What's this?'

Most of the plan was clear. The outlines of the flowerbeds, walls and paths were all carefully drawn in. But in one place there was nothing. Just blank white paper.

'Look.' Kate pointed towards the bottom of the garden, to the biggest of the remaining mounds of brambles. 'I think I know what's under there. It's what Walter was going to look for when he . . . when he got ill.' She paused. 'I thought we could try to do that bit this afternoon,' she went on. 'I want to show you all the plants I've found first.'

Kate had already cleared and forked the soil around many of the plants. She had carried compost from the old heaps on the far side of the garden, and fat green shoots were growing everywhere. Louise laughed at some of the things Kate had marked. 'That's a thistle,' she said, 'and that one's a baby sycamore tree. But these others look interesting.'

'I worked out what some of them are,' Kate said. 'But they don't show you what they look like when they're small. I hope the library people don't mind a bit of dirt on their books.' Louise looked at the state of the book in Kate's hand. 'Yeah, well,' Kate grinned, 'Dad says we can always buy them another copy.'

By the time Dad appeared to tell them that lunch was ready, Kate and Louise had worked their way nearly to the bottom of the garden. Mike and his friends had been making slow progress with the lawn. One of them had taken the mower to bits and was carefully cleaning the parts. The others stood up and groaned as they inspected the blisters on their hands. Kate looked down at her own hands. The skin was hard and callused. Dirt had worked into every crack, and they were covered with tiny cuts and scratches. All the hard work she had done written there, far clearer than words.

From somewhere, Dad had produced a mountain of pizza. It disappeared incredibly fast. 'Is that mower going to work, then?' Kate asked James, the boy who was trying to fix it. His face was streaked with rust and oil. He grinned at Kate.

'I don't see why not,' he said. 'I'm nearly ready to try it out.' He swallowed the last of his pizza and picked up a spanner.

'So what do you think's under that clump of brambles?' Louise asked Kate.

'I'm not telling you,' Kate said. 'Not till we find it. Come on.'

They made their way back to the end of the garden and began to slash at the undergrowth. They were out of sight of the main part of the garden here, and the boys' voices could hardly be heard. Emily wanted to help, but the thorns were wickedly sharp, and she had to sit on the grass and watch. Slowly the girls hacked a passageway into the thicket. Then they heard the clink of metal on stone. 'Here,' said Kate. 'Look!'

She pulled back some trailing stems and Louise saw the beginning of a low wall. 'Pass me the spade,' said Kate. She thrust the blade into the undergrowth at their feet and there was another scraping sound. 'This is it, all right,' she said. 'Paving stones, see? It won't take long now. You see up there?' She pointed to where the brambles rose high above their heads. 'There's a kind of arch that goes over the top. Or there was. And there used to be roses growing on it. This bit here should be a sort of circle. And there's a seat at the back. Look.' Kate pulled a faded photograph from her pocket. 'I found this in the back of Walter's book. I think this must be the place.'

The photograph showed a young, smiling Walter sitting on a bench with his arms around a laughing woman in a flowery dress. Red roses climbed over the arch above their heads. Louise stood looking at the picture for a long time, then she said, 'Wouldn't it be brilliant if the roses were still here?'

'Can you tell a rose from a bramble?' Kate asked.

Louise took the cutters and began to snip away pieces of bramble until she found the beginning of the metal arch. Several times she exclaimed as thorns pierced her thick gloves, but at last she said, 'Here! Come and see.'

The stem Louise had found was nearly as thick as her wrist. 'It's going to be hard to cut away the brambles without cutting the rose,' she said, 'but you have to prune roses anyhow, so if we do cut some of it down I don't suppose it will matter.'

Louise and Kate worked on through the afternoon, hardly noticing the sound of the lawnmower or the excited laughter of the boys, or Pups barking madly. They cleared two shallow stone steps that led down into a paved circle with a stone seat at the back of it. The rose arched over the top like a roof. Finally, they could do no more and they both flopped down on the bench.

'Emily!' exclaimed Kate. 'What have you done?'

Emily had excavated a huge hole in the grass. 'That's the lawn!' yelled Kate. 'You've got your own garden to dig in.'

'I didn't dig.' Emily's face crumpled. 'The hole was here.'

'I'm sorry,' said Kate quickly. 'I didn't mean to shout. Let's have a look.'

Emily's hole was very odd. It was about a metre wide, quite shallow, and lined with stone or concrete. Suddenly, Louise said, 'I know what this is! It's a bird bath. I remember it. I don't remember anything else, but I remember this. I used to sit very quietly and watch the birds come and wash themselves. It was like a little pond.'

'Can we fill it up?' Emily pleaded. 'Please?'

They set off for the house. When they turned the corner they were amazed. The expanse of grass in front of them didn't look much like a lawn, but it was flat. Well, flat-*ish*. And it seemed huge. James was just pushing the mower over the last little bit. Pups was following him, wagging his tail. The rest of the boys were lying exhausted on the ground. 'It's fantastic,' said Kate. 'You really could have a game of footie on it.' None of them moved.

'It was torture,' groaned Darren. 'It was worse than training.'

'It doesn't look like that on the TV,' said Nathan. 'It looks like it's not work at all. You don't see their hands bleeding.'

'We'd never have done it if James hadn't fixed the mower,' said Mike.

'Good Lord!' Dad exclaimed. 'I wouldn't have thought it was possible. It looks like a real garden.'

He was standing at the edge of the path. His overalls were covered in tile cement. The sun was sinking behind the trees, and as the long shadows fell across the ragged grass, the imperfections seemed to disappear. The boys stood up and stared at what they'd done. And at what Kate and Louise had done. Because with the tangled grass flattened they could see the flowerbeds on the far side, with their neat edging, and the tall shrubs, free of brambles

172

now, overhanging the beds. Sunlight filtered through the bushes and lit up the carpet of bluebells under the old tree, so that the deepening blue of the sky seemed to be reflected there. A silence fell on all of them. Pheasants called and flapped in the field beyond the garden, and something swooped past Kate's face, turned, and zipped through the middle of the group of boys.

'It's a bat,' whispered Mike. The bat made a couple of circuits of the garden and then flitted out of sight.

'It likes the garden,' said Kate.

'I don't blame it,' said Dad.

Later, when the boys had left, the telephone rang. Dad answered it, and Kate knew at once that it was Mum. She edged closer to listen. At first Dad just said, 'Yes' or 'No'. Then Kate heard him telling Mum how she had learned to read. He was telling her how she could use the computer. For a second, she thought he was going to tell her about school, and her heart started to thump. Dad saw her face. He gave her the thumbs-up sign. 'Mum's really pleased,' he said. 'Here. Talk to her.' Dad held out the phone.

Dad was right. Mum's words tumbled over each other as she told Kate how wonderful it was. ' It's such a weight off my mind,' she said. 'All this time I've been so worried about you. And it sounds like he's really getting on with the house.'

Kate was suddenly desperate to see Mum. She couldn't stand having so many things she couldn't tell her. It felt all wrong. What was the point in putting it off any longer? Anyone could see that the garden was going to be fantastic. Anyone could see that Dad was getting the house sorted. And if Mum couldn't see *now* that she was better off not going to school, well, would she ever? 'We've been doing lots of things,' she said. 'Why don't you come and see? Please.'

There was a long pause. Then Mum said, 'I don't think I'm ready for that yet. I mean, it's great that it's all going so well. And I'm really missing you . . .'

'Then come.'

'I can't, love. Not yet. I told Dad. I think we should meet up in London. At Easter. I thought Easter Sunday. We could all go and do something. A trip on the river, maybe. Come on, Kate. Say something. Don't tell me you've gone off London.'

And suddenly, the thought that Kate kept trying not to think was there, right in front of her, blocking out the light. *What if it's all a waste of time? What if none of it works? What if Mum and Dad never . . . ?*

She put the phone down and stumbled outside into the garden.

Chapter 16

Kate had never felt so nervous. She looked across at Mike. He was curled up in the corner of the back seat of the car, buried in a book as usual. But he had read the same page about four times now. He looked up and caught her eye. It was obvious that he was feeling the same way as she was.

Kate was holding two exercise books. Dad had been furious when she had refused to bring the garden book to show Mum. 'Can't you see?' he had said. 'It's the one thing that'll make her believe that it's OK, you not

176

going to school. No-one could argue with something like that.'

'I want the garden to be a surprise. That's the whole point. If Mum sees drawings and plans and photos, it won't be, will it?'

'If I'd known you were going to do this, I wouldn't have . . . I'm almost starting to feel sorry for those teachers of yours. Oh well. You'll just have to bring your maths and English books.'

Dad had been to Norwich and bought some text books for Kate to work from, but she hadn't had time to do much. Most of her effort had gone into the garden diary. And that was the one thing she couldn't show Mum. That would spoil everything.

'We don't have to tell her now,' Kate had said.

'Yes, we do. It's one thing not telling her on the phone. When we see her, I'm going to *have* to tell her. You must see that.'

In the front seat, Dad was humming along to a Beatles tape. He only ever hummed when he was worried. The Beatles tape was Mum's favourite. They were stuck behind another tractor. They'd been driving for over an hour now, and they were still miles away from the motorway. So far, they'd been stuck behind four tractors and a milk tanker. Dad looked at his watch again.

'I knew we should have left earlier. Once we get to the motorway, it's another hour to London. And then if the traffic's bad . . . You know what Mum'll be like if we're late.'

Dad put his foot down and swerved past the tractor.

Kate closed her eyes and thought about Walter. They had been to see him the day before. Kate had been bubbling with news about the garden.

'All Mike's friends have been helping. The first day they were totally out of it. Exhausted. I never thought they'd come back, but they did. We've been working all week. It looks fantastic, doesn't it Mike?'

Mike nodded doubtfully. He was looking at Walter's face. Walter seemed far away. He didn't appear to be listening to what Kate was saying. She kept talking. 'Even the grass has started to grow. It looked bad at first. Just all browny yellow stalks. But there's loads of little shoots coming up since it rained. I bet in a few weeks it'll be a perfect lawn. And Dad's going to buy a new mower, aren't you, Dad?'

'Sure,' said Dad. 'When the cash comes through.' Dad had been right about the work coming in. He had been working on the house during the day, and staying up half the night working on the computer. Kate kept talking.

'And I've been weeding your vegetable garden every day with Louise. Everything's getting huge. When you get home, there won't be anything needs doing. And we'll keep on looking after it for you.'

'I'm not going back.' Walter said. He reached out a thin brown hand and stroked Emily's hair.

'What?'

Walter had spoken quietly. It took a moment for his words to register.

'I can't go back. Look at me. I'm too weak. I don't reckon I could even walk down the path.'

'But you can't just stay here.'

Walter smiled and tried to hoist himself up against the pillows. 'Let me,' said Dad.

'See?' said Walter. 'Weak as a kitten.'

'But what . . . ?'

'I'm going to one of them homes.'

'But you said . . . ?'

'I know what I said.' Walter spoke sharply, and for a second Kate saw a flash of the old Walter. It didn't last. 'I en't got no choice, have I?'

'But you'll hate it there. You . . .'

'That's enough, Kate,' said Dad. There was a silence. Walter closed his eyes and Emily held

179

his hand. After a moment he opened his eyes again.

'I'm glad you've done the garden,' he said. 'I'd like to see that. And maybe you could bring me some vegetables. Some of them carrots should be ready by now.'

'We'll take photographs,' said Kate. 'Mike's good at that. We'll bring them and show you. And we'll bring you all sorts of things.'

'Let's see them green fingers of yours,' said Walter. Kate held out a hand and Walter took it in his own and turned it over. He ran his leathery fingers over the hard calluses and scars on Kate's palm; at the soil that no amount of scrubbing could remove from around her nails. 'Done some work, haven't they?' he said. Kate nodded.

'Come and see me,' Walter said. 'I don't care about pictures. I can see it all, clear as day, in my mind. Just you come and see me.'

'I will,' promised Kate.

'Look there!' said Mike, as the motorway swept over the hilltop, through rolling fields. 'Canary Wharf. We're nearly there.'

'You still haven't told us where we're meeting Mum,' said Kate.

'I'm not going to either,' said Dad. 'It's a surprise. And we've still got quite a way to go.'

And then the fields were gone and there were houses on every side. Factories, concrete. Cars and people everywhere. The smell of the city filtered into the car. Exhaust fumes, dust. A few months ago Kate would have thought this was the smell of home. Now, as they drove past cinemas, tube stations and giant super-markets, Kate wondered how she had ever survived here. At the top of a hill they passed a long wire fence and a row of trees beside a superstore. Tattered plastic shopping bags clung to every inch of the fence, and to every branch of every tree.

'Well,' said Dad, looking anxiously at his watch, 'at least we've left all this behind.'

'Kew Gardens!' said Kate as Dad parked the car beside the river. 'Brilliant, Dad!'

'I thought you'd like it. We're meeting Mum in the café at 12.00, so we'll have to run.'

The gardens were vast. When they came through the hedge from the car-park Kate couldn't believe her eyes. She had expected, well, gardens. Not a huge park stretching away into the distance. It seemed crazy to drive all the way to London only to find yourself in the country again. Dad lifted Emily onto his shoulders and set off down the path.

'Hey, look,' said Mike. 'The trees have got labels.'

Sure enough, each tree had a metal label hanging from it. Kate began trying to decipher one, but Dad dragged her away. 'No time now,' he said. 'Later on.'

As they entered the café Kate felt her heart thumping. The café was big, and it was crowded. Then she heard Mum's voice. 'Over here!'

Kate turned and saw Mum's battered denim jacket. That was the only thing about her that looked the same. Mum's long, curly red hair had gone. Well, most of it had gone. And it wasn't red any more. It was black. Mum's face looked different, too. Something about the make-up, maybe. But one thing Kate was sure of. Mum was as nervous as any of them. Kate and Emily hugged her tightly, and Kate couldn't stop herself crying, but she hid her face in Mum's jacket. And there was another thing. A new perfume. She heard Mum say, 'Hello, Mike.' Mike mumbled something Kate couldn't hear.

'What have you done to your hair?' said Dad. His voice sounded odd, as if it wasn't working properly.

'I knew it . . .' Mum began.

Kate couldn't bear it. 'Don't!' she said.

'Please, don't.' She let go of Mum and stepped back. 'I think your hair looks great,' she said, 'and we're all starving. We are going to have lunch here, aren't we?'

'You bet,' said Dad. 'Let's spend some of my hard-earned cash.' He looked at Mum. 'The business is really taking off,' he said. 'I got a big cheque in the post yesterday.'

Kate hardly tasted her lunch. The air was filled with the things Mum and Dad weren't saying to each other. Kate told Mum about Walter. She found herself saying more and more about the garden. It was impossible to talk about Walter without talking about the garden.

'Well, I'm glad you've been getting some fresh air and exercise,' Mum said. 'I can't imagine you getting very far with that jungle, though.'

'But we . . .' Mike began. Kate kicked him hard under the table.

'You're probably right,' Kate said.

'I'm sure I am. Now tell me. About school. I just *knew* it was a good school. When Dad told me you'd learned to read, I nearly rang them up straight away to congratulate them. The teachers must be fantastic . . .' Mum saw the expression on Kate's and Dad's faces, and stopped. 'What?' she said.

Kate couldn't speak.

'There isn't an easy way to say this,' said Dad. 'Kate's not been going to school.'

'I don't understand. You said . . .'

'I've been teaching her at home. Something happened at school. And I . . . we . . . decided it was best.'

Mum stared at them. Her face was grim. 'And you didn't bother to tell me? Well, no, I suppose you wouldn't. My God, Dave. You've done some stupid things, but . . .'

'Now just hang on a minute,' said Dad. Kate had been staring at the floor. Now, something in Dad's voice made her look up. There was the same strength in him that she had seen when Walter was taken ill. And in Mrs Denby's office. 'It's not as simple as it seems,' Dad went on. 'I'd have reacted just the same way . . .'

'I bet!' said Mum.

'Yeah, well. Why don't you let me explain?'

'Yes, why don't you? This should be good.'

'Go on, Kate,' Dad said. 'Take the others outside. By those big pools. We'll meet you there. And leave me those books.' Dad took the books and squeezed Kate's hand. 'Off you go,' he said. 'It'll be fine.' Kate didn't dare look at Mum.

Mike took Emily off to play on the grass. Kate sat on a bench. She had no idea how long she sat there in the sun, watching people pass by, before she heard Mum's voice.

'Kate?' Mum sat down beside her. Dad had joined Mike and Emily on the grass. 'You did all this?' Mum was holding the exercise books. Kate nodded. 'And you really learned to read on your own? It wasn't school?'

'Mum, I hate school. I've always hated it. It makes me feel ill. When I'm there, I can't do anything. But I love making things grow. I love looking after things that are growing. I don't *know* how I learned to read. I just did. But it *definitely* wasn't school.'

Mum didn't say anything. She was watching Dad playing with Emily and Mike. She blinked. 'I don't know what to think about all this, Kate. I mean, what are you going to do with your life? What about exams? What . . . ?'

'You worry too much,' said Dad. He had Emily on his shoulders. He was out of breath, and grinning. Mum was leafing through Kate's books again. 'All sorted?' asked Dad.

'I never thought I'd see you do anything like this,' said Mum. 'So I suppose it must be all right . . .' Kate flung her arms around her. 'Hold on. I haven't finished. We'll leave things as they are for the moment. Whatever you've

185

been doing, it seems to be working. And then maybe in September . . .'

'Thanks, Mum,' said Kate. September seemed a very long way in the future. And before then Mum would have seen the garden and the house.

'See?' Dad said to Kate. 'I told you it was a good idea to bring the evidence. Now, let's go and look at the gardens. It would be a shame to come all this way and not see anything.'

Near the café there were several enormous greenhouses. Inside, the air was steamy and the plants towered above them. 'It's an indoor jungle,' Mike said. 'And look! You can go up in the tree-tops.'

A spiral staircase climbed up among the palm trees. 'Come on,' said Mike. Kate started to follow him up the stairs.

'Me too,' said Emily.

'I don't think I can,' said Mum, looking up. 'I can't stand heights.'

'Here,' said Kate. 'Hold my hand, Emily.'

'Be careful,' Dad warned. 'Don't let her run off. Watch out for snakes.'

Emily stopped and looked back in alarm.

'Only joking,' Dad laughed. 'Go on, you lot. I'm staying down here with Mum. We've got things to talk about.'

They walked along the narrow platform. The

186

tops of the palm trees seemed to be trying to force their way out through the glass. Emily suddenly dashed away from them. 'I'm winning!' she yelled. Mike went after her. Kate looked down and saw Mum and Dad sitting on a bench. Her heart lurched terribly as she saw that they were sitting very close together, holding hands, talking. Emily's voice cried out excitedly from the far end of the jungle.

'Mum! Look at me!'

Two faces turned upwards at the same moment. Kate was close enough to see that both of them were crying.

They gave Mum a lift home. Kathy's house was in the next street to the one where they used to live. As they drove down the High Street Kate saw a bunch of kids kicking a cardboard box around outside the tube station. With a shock she recognized Yasmin and Suzy. They looked taller, more grown-up. The traffic lights at the corner were red. Suzy glanced over at their car, and without thinking, Kate slid lower in her seat, so she couldn't be seen.

Mum and Dad were silent in the front of the car. Something had changed between them. Kate could see that. But she couldn't tell exactly what it was that had changed. Or whether it was good or bad. There was still a distance between them, but it was a different kind of distance, something like respect. And why had they been crying? Because something had ended? Because . . . ?'

'Hey, Emily,' said Mum. 'What do you want for your birthday? It's not long now. It'll be June before you know it.' They were the first words Mum had spoken since they had left Kew.

'I want a spade,' said Emily at once, 'and my own wheelbarrow. And I want a party. I want everyone to come. I want all my friends and I want Walter and Louise.'

Kate saw Mum and Dad look at each other.

'Well?' said Dad.

'Can I come too?' asked Mum.

'Don't be silly,' said Emily. 'You have to make the cake.'

Summer

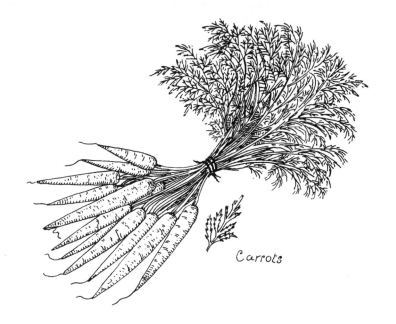

Carrots

Chapter 17

A few weeks later, Walter moved to a home.

'It's not too bad,' said Louise, when Kate asked her about it. 'I went on Sunday and I stayed all day. We just talked, like we used to when I was little. And I found out the most amazing thing. I always thought Grandad had never been anywhere. It turns out he went all over the world in the war. He even went to America. I don't know why he never told me before.'

The following weekend, Dad drove them to the Clifftop Retirement Home. It was in a small seaside town. 'I didn't know the sea was so close,' said Kate as they turned a corner and caught a glimpse of blue through the trees.

'You should have looked at the map,' Dad replied. 'And speaking of maps, what's happened to the navigation? Which way now?

The home was right at the edge of the town, a cluster of low buildings with a large car-park in front of it. Kate hated it at once, before they had even gone inside. A nurse directed them to a big room where a television was showing some kind of quiz show. About twenty old men and women in wheelchairs sat in a circle. None of them was watching the TV. Some were asleep. None of them was Walter.

'Over there,' said Mike. Walter was sitting in a high-backed chair by the window, gazing out at a small patch of grass. Louise was sitting beside him. His face lit up when he saw them.

'Look at that robin,' he said. 'Me and Louise have been watching him. Look there! He's back again. He'd hop right inside if they'd let me open a window. But I reckon a breath of fresh air would kill half of this lot.'

As he spoke, an old man on the far side of the room began singing in a cracked voice. *'You are my sunshine, my only sunshine . . .'*

'He do that all day,' said Walter, leaning towards them. 'He hardly ever stop.'

Walter definitely looked better, Kate thought. Not miserable and scared like he'd been in hospital. After a while, Emily climbed onto Walter's knee. 'I'm having a party,' she said. 'Here's your invitation.' She handed Walter the piece of paper covered with brightly coloured scribble that she'd been working on all morning. Walter examined it carefully.

'That don't say when it is,' he said finally.

'Yes it does,' said Emily, pointing to a big red squiggle. 'There. The sixth of June. And you have to reply. You always have to reply. At Nursery, they just give them to you, but *you'll* have to write a letter.'

'You will come, won't you?' Kate said to Walter. 'You can see the garden and everything. There's no reason not to come.'

'I don't know.' Walter looked away out of the window. He wouldn't meet her eyes. 'I don't know if I can.'

'Look, Grandad,' said Louise. 'There's the robin again.'

'Come on, Kate,' said Dad. 'Time to go.'

The next day, Kate walked across the fields to Louise's house. Mr Fuller looked up from the engine of an enormous tractor as Kate arrived in the yard. 'Kate,' he called down, 'shouldn't

193

you be at school? Oh, no. Louise told me. So how's it going?'

'It's about Walter,' said Kate. 'Please. You've got to help.'

Kate told Mr Fuller about Emily's party.

'I'd like to see this garden myself. I always felt a bit bad about that. Letting it go, you know. But Debbie wanted something new. Anyway, what did Walter say when you gave him this invitation?'

'He said he wasn't sure. But he wants to, really. He probably thinks you'll worry about him going out. But if you tell him it's all right . . .'

'You do know, don't you,' said Mr Fuller gently, 'that Walter isn't going to come back and live in his cottage again.' Kate was silent. 'That's why it might upset him to come back here. He's made his decision, you see. And it wasn't easy.'

'But it wasn't him who decided, was it?' said Kate angrily. 'You made him go into that place.' Kate stopped. She was making a mess of this. 'I'm sorry,' she said. 'I didn't mean it.'

'Yes, you did. And I know how you feel. But, you know, Clifftop isn't bad as those places go and, believe me, we've seen plenty. We simply couldn't keep an eye on him all the time. You know that, don't you?'

'In the garden,' Kate said. 'I didn't want him to start cutting things down, but he just started. I couldn't stop him.'

Mr Fuller didn't seem to have really heard her. 'We couldn't go on the way we were, Kate,' he continued. 'None of us could. But you mustn't be upset. Walter's being properly cared for now, and he could live for years.'

'I suppose so.'

'Really. He's very fond of you.'

Kate looked up, startled and embarrassed. Mr Fuller laughed. 'You're very like him, you know,' he said. 'Look, I'll do my best to get him to your sister's party. Only, it has to be what *he* wants, OK?' Kate nodded. 'Oh, and I was going to tell you earlier. I was talking to the people at the home. I told them about Walter's garden. All these vegetables and no-one to eat them. They were very interested. They'll take all you can spare.'

'But . . .'

'They'll pay you, of course. You don't want all your hard work to go to waste, do you?'

Kate shook her head.

'And what's more,' added Mr Fuller with a broad grin, 'Walter won't be able to complain about the food, will he?'

Even Kate had to laugh at that.

*   *   *

They were having breakfast when the postman came. He didn't bother with the box at the front these days. He just pushed open the newly painted back door and came in.

'Miss Emily Oakley,' he said, holding out the letter. 'I reckon that's from Walter.'

Emily grabbed the letter. She'd been waiting for it more impatiently with each day that passed. She ripped open the envelope and thrust the letter at Mike, but before he could take it, Kate snatched it away.

'He's going to come!' she said. 'I knew he would.'

'This'll be the big party, then?' said the postman.

'It's *my* party,' Emily said, 'and *everybody's* coming.'

Kate went out into the garden. The lawn really looked like a lawn now. Dad had bought a powerful new mower and Mike had been cutting the grass every chance he had. But it was the flowers and shrubs that were truly amazing. On the wall of the house, a honeysuckle was blooming, filling the air with perfume. The *Philadelphus*, the first plant Walter had shown her, was full of tiny white buds. Any day now they would burst open. And, on the old metal arch over the stone seat, the climbing rose was about to bloom. There were flowers, or the promise of flowers, everywhere.

In a special sunny patch of flowerbed, Kate had made a home for the *Cosmos* plants that Walter had given her on the day he had rescued them from the cows. Yesterday, she had planted them out, and now she gave each of them a little water, then stood up and looked around. She remembered how she had stood here, right here, with Mum on a February night as the stars came out. This was what Mum had wanted. She remembered the day they had come to look at the house for the very first time. It was only because of the garden that Mum had agreed to buy the house.

There was only a week to wait. Then Mum would be here. Mum had been phoning every night, having long conversations with Dad. Kate couldn't understand how it had happened, but being apart seemed to have made Mum and Dad more *themselves*. And now, at last, they were talking to each other. In spite of everything, in spite of the fear in her heart, Kate felt hope returning.

Kate was up very early on the day of Emily's party. Pups opened one eye and looked at her from his basket as she went through the kitchen. He was an old dog, Kate had realized,

197

and he didn't like getting up too early.

She wandered into the garden and stood in the middle of the lawn. Everything was still. Every blade of grass, every leaf, had its own tiny droplet of dew. The sky was bright in the east and the long bands of cloud were already being touched by the sun that had not yet risen. Birds began to sing. First one, then more and more. The robin hopped close to her feet, pecking in the damp grass. Then he fluttered off and dipped his beak in the bird pond that Emily had found. Kate smiled to herself. The birds hadn't been able to use it much. It was Emily's favourite place in the garden. Kate heard footsteps behind her. Mike was walking across the terrace with Emily holding his hand. Pups came out of the door and flopped down on the flagstones.

'It's my party today,' Emily said, 'isn't it?'

'Yes,' said Mike and Kate together.

'And Mum's going to make me a cake, isn't she?'

'Yes,' said Mike and Kate.

'It's going to be OK,' Mike told Kate. 'Mum's going to love everything. How could she not be impressed?'

Kate didn't reply.

Right after breakfast, Dad drove to the station with Emily and Mike.

'I don't want to come,' said Kate.

'Sure?' Kate could see from the look on Dad's face that he knew what she was feeling. And whatever she was feeling, Dad must be feeling it worse.

'I want to see Mum's face when she sees the garden,' she said. 'I want that to be the first thing. And I have to go and help Louise with the vegetables, too.'

Kate watched the car go, and then walked down the lane to Walter's cottage with Pups beside her. Creamy clouds of cow parsley overhung the verges. Louise had told her what it was called, and she'd thought she was joking at first. Kate knew the names of the trees now, too. The ones that had looked like bony people in the winter were oaks. They stood in the hedgerows covered with new leaves. On the corner, by the church, were tall grey ash trees. Kate reached Walter's garden just as the cows arrived. She skipped quickly inside the gate. Pups leaped up and licked Louise's face.

'You're not still scared of them, are you?' said Louise. 'You see them every day.'

'I can't help it,' said Kate.

'You used to be scared of Pups,' said Louise. 'And look at you now.' She was digging up carrots.

Kate took the basket from her and began

washing them under the tap. 'Cows are different,' she said.

'Dad says they want a box of lettuces, and as many carrots as we've got,' Louise told her. 'We'll take them when we collect Walter for the party.'

They worked until they had several bunches of carrots neatly tied with string around their feathery green leaves.

'I'd better go,' said Kate. 'I've got to be there when they get back.'

'Shall I come with you? There's time. We're not collecting Grandad until this afternoon.'

Kate hesitated. The garden was almost as much Louise's as it was hers. She could never have done it without Louise. But this moment had been in her mind for so long now. Her and Mum in the garden on their own . . .

'It's OK,' Louise said, understanding. 'I'll see you later, at the party. And Kate . . .' Kate looked back as she opened the gate. 'Good luck.'

Kate heard the car doors slam at the front of the house. She didn't see Mum's astonishment at the clean sweep of shingle where the rubbish heaps had been, and she didn't see Dad holding back Mike and Emily as Mum walked round the side of the house.

'Kate? Where are you?'

Kate heard Mum's voice. She heard footsteps on the gravel. And then Mum was there. Her mouth fell open and her hands flew to her face, just the way it always was on the programmes on the TV. Mum crossed to the edge of the terrace and began to walk down the steps. Kate still couldn't move. Then Mum swayed slightly, and Kate ran to her.

'Mum! What is it?'

Mum sat on the top step, and stared. Kate sat beside her and Mum hugged her. 'I can't believe it,' she said. 'It's like a dream.'

'It's real all right,' said Mike. Dad hadn't been able to hold them back any longer. 'And when we were doing it, it was like a nightmare.'

'No it wasn't,' said Kate. 'You enjoyed it. You all did.'

Mum stood up and they walked together around the edge of the lawn. Kate told Mum the names of all the plants. Mike and Emily soon got bored and started practising handstands on the grass.

'You like it, then?' said Kate, when they reached the far end of the garden. They sat down on the bench.

'Don't be silly,' said Mum. Kate could see she was trying not to cry. 'It's the most beautiful thing I've ever seen. You must have worked so hard. I don't know what to say.'

'You could . . .' Kate stopped. From the look in Mum's eyes, Kate knew that Mum knew what she was about to say. Mum shook her head.

'Don't, Kate. Don't ask me. Not now, OK? Not yet.' And suddenly, Kate found herself clinging to Mum, and sobbing. She couldn't help herself. She couldn't stop. She heard the birds singing. She felt Mum's hand stroking her hair. She heard Mike and Emily playing, laughing, and it seemed as if they were in another world. Gradually her sobs subsided.

'I've missed you, Mum,' Kate said.

'Me too,' said Mum. 'Now dry your eyes. This is Emily's day and we've got to make it special for her, OK? Whatever we feel like inside.'

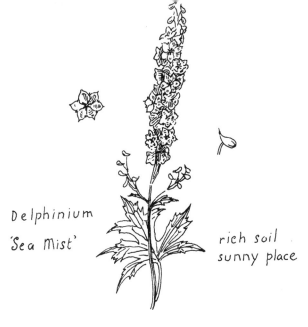

Delphinium
'Sea Mist'

rich soil
sunny place

Chapter 18

Mum couldn't speak when she saw the kitchen. Dad had polished everything that morning, and he'd hoovered the entire house as well. Mum walked around the room in a daze, opening cupboards, running her hands over the newly tiled surfaces.

'And it's not just the kitchen, either,' said Dad. 'Would you like to see the rest of the house?' Mum explored, and they all followed behind. Kate realized that everything had changed since Mum had gone away. The house had changed, the garden had changed. *They* had all changed. It was as if Mum was a stranger in the house, a guest being shown around. Dad didn't say anything as they went from room to room. Not until they reached the living room, the site of the great fireplace disaster.

'Good Lord!' said Mum. 'What's that?'

It wasn't the new fireplace that astonished Mum. It was Dad's new stereo system. The speakers looked as though they belonged to a rock band. They were taller than Emily.

'Yeah, well.' Dad grinned sheepishly. 'I could never play music really loud in the flat. But round here there's no-one to complain. Except the cows. And they don't seem to mind. Listen.'

Dad picked up the remote, and music filled the room. The Beatles. Drums getting louder and louder until the sound was deafening – but brilliant at the same time.

Mum laughed then, and Kate saw a look pass between her and Dad that she hadn't seen for a long time.

Mum had brought Emily's birthday cake in a huge box, but she wouldn't show them. 'It's a surprise,' was all she would say. And then she began to make biscuits and buns. She made the special 'Melting Moments' that they all loved, with cherries on top. She made round, buttery biscuits, and fat, delicious buns. Dad was a good cook, but he never did baking. That was Mum's thing. They all sat around the big oak table, Dad included, and watched – and smelt. While she baked, Mum asked questions. Bit by bit, they told her everything properly. Dad had photocopied Walter's photograph of the garden, and it was hanging on the wall. Mum looked at it carefully.

'Go on then, Kate,' said Dad. 'What are you waiting for?'

Kate had been holding the book in her hands all the time they had been talking. Her book. She held it out to Mum.

'What's this?' Mum wiped her floury hands on her apron and took the book. When Kate didn't answer, couldn't answer, Mum began to turn the pages. After a few moments she looked up. 'You wrote all this? You drew the pictures? Everything?' Kate nodded. Mum turned the pages slowly, completely absorbed. 'It's wonderful, Kate,' she said, when she reached the end. 'It's amazing. You . . .'

Kate felt her face growing hot. She saw Mike and Emily staring at her. She pushed Walter's diary across the table. 'Look,' she said. 'This is what gave me the idea.'

Mum understood. She put Kate's book down reluctantly, and opened Walter's diary. She gazed at the faded, old-fashioned handwriting.

'It's very sad,' she said at last. 'It's so lovely here. He must really miss it. I do hope it's a good idea, him coming back.'

'He wanted to,' said Kate. 'Emily asked him, and he wrote and said he'd come.'

'Well,' said Mum, 'it will be nice to meet him properly. I didn't much like the look of him the first time I saw him.'

Then there was loads to do to get ready for the party. Kate made the parcel for pass the parcel. 'You'll need lots of layers, 'cos there's lots of people,' Emily told her. 'And there must be a sweet in *every* layer.' She watched like a hawk to make sure Kate did as she was told. Kate kept sneaking glances at Mum and Dad as she worked. She knew it was stupid, that it was too soon, but she couldn't help looking for signs. And the best sign of all was that, so far, they hadn't argued about anything. Mike was icing clowns' faces onto biscuits. He looked up, caught Kate's eye, and smiled.

The party was in full swing when Walter arrived. Marty and the postman were playing musical bumps on the grass with Emily and all her friends from the playgroup. Kate had just finished carrying plates of sandwiches outside when Louise appeared.

'Mum and Dad are just getting him out of the car. Come on.'

Kate followed her. There were several cars in the lane, and the Fullers had parked quite a way from the house. She heard the sound of Pups barking. With so many people around, Mum and Dad had decided it was best to keep him safely inside. Louise's mum was trying to persuade Walter to get into a wheelchair.

'I haven't lost the use of my legs,' he said, 'not yet, I haven't.'

Kate was alarmed at how frail Walter looked. She saw the worry on Mrs Fuller's face.

'You can't walk all that way, Walter,' Kate said. Mrs Fuller smiled gratefully at her.

'See, Dad? Even Kate thinks you should ride.'

So Walter lowered himself, still grumbling, into the wheelchair, and Kate pushed him along the lane and into the garden. 'There!' she said, as they turned the corner. 'What do you think?'

'Grandad?' said Louise. 'Say something.'

Walter stared at the garden, the wide path leading on to the terrace, the steps down to the lawn where the children were playing, the flowerbeds overhung by tall bushes and trees. 'I don't believe it,' he said, finally. He shook his head in amazement. 'I just don't believe it.' He started to heave himself out of the wheelchair, but Kate placed a gentle hand on his shoulder. 'I don't feel right in this thing,' he grumbled. 'I want to feel the ground under my feet.'

'Come on, Grandad,' said Louise. 'Just a bit further.'

Walter started to argue, but then Emily appeared, pushing her new wheelbarrow. She parked the wheelbarrow beside the wheelchair, climbed up on Walter's lap, and kissed him. 'Would you like to come and play musical bumps?' she said. 'This is my new wheelbarrow. I've got my own garden. Would you like to see it? I like your buggy. I had one like that, but I don't need it any more. My mummy's come home.'

'Happy birthday,' said Walter. He handed Emily the small parcel he was holding. Emily ripped off the paper. Inside there were two packets of seeds. 'Thank you,' said Emily. 'Please will you help me plant them in my garden?'

Walter smiled. 'Course I will,' he said, 'if they'll let me out of this thing for a minute.'

Kate wheeled Walter along the edge of the lawn, past the squealing children playing musical bumps. 'All right, Walter?' panted Marty, jumping up and down in time to the music.

Walter smiled and nodded. He could hardly take his eyes off the flowerbeds. He greeted the plants as if they were old friends. 'Look there!'

he said, as they passed a tall clump of pale blue delphiniums. 'That's called *Sea Mist*. Margaret loved that one. And look over there. That's . . .'

'This is *my* garden,' said Emily proudly as they arrived at a small patch of brown earth.

'Ah,' said Walter. Emily's worm searches and mud pie making hadn't done her garden much good. Kate and Louise helped Walter out of the wheelchair. 'That's no use,' he said, as he stood holding on to them. 'Let me get down there. Can't do nothing from up here, can I?'

Kate looked at Louise's mum and dad. 'Go on then,' said Mrs Fuller. 'I don't see what harm it can do. At least you can't fall over.'

Louise and Kate helped Walter carefully down onto his knees. At one point, Kate felt his whole weight on her arms. She was amazed at how light he was.

'Pass me your fork,' he said to Emily. She handed him the little fork that Kate had given her for her birthday. Walter began to dig, lifting and smoothing the soil, ready for the seeds. When everything was ready, Emily sprinkled the seeds in the ground, and Walter gently covered them up.

'There!' he said, when they had helped him to his feet again. 'That'll do. Now I want a proper look at the rest of the garden. I want to see everything, mind.'

Kate and Louise led Walter along the edge of the flowerbeds, and then they turned the corner and Walter saw the stone seat, and the roses. Only the week before, the first buds had opened, and now the arch was covered with flowers. Kate felt Walter's hand squeeze her shoulder tightly. She looked up, and saw the tears in his eyes.

'We used to sit there in the evenings,' he said, after a long moment. 'We'd come out and watch the birds. They'd all come if we sat quiet enough.'

'There's a picture,' said Kate. 'I found it. It was in your book.'

She pulled the photograph from her pocket and handed to Walter. He looked at it, and then he smiled. 'Come you on,' he said. 'You'd better show me the rest.'

When they finally arrived back at the terrace, Walter sat down in the warm sunshine. 'I never thought you'd do it,' he said. 'I reckoned me and Marty'd do most of it. You sure he didn't help?'

'Hi, Walter,' said Dad. 'They did it themselves, I promise you. Just the kids. I never met anyone who knew as much about plants as your Louise. Well, except maybe Kate now.'

'Hello, there,' said Mum. 'You must be Walter. I'm Sarah.' Mum was holding a bottle of champagne in one hand, and a bowl of crisps in the other. 'The children are all happy now. But I thought the grown-ups could have this instead of lemonade.'

'Grandad?' said Louise. 'Grandad! What is it?' Walter was staring at Mum. He blinked and shook his head. 'I'm all right,' he said. 'Don't you worry about me.' He smiled at Mum, and started to get up.

'No, no,' said Mum. She put down the bottle and reached over to shake Walter's hand. Dad came up behind her with a tray of glasses.

'Right, then,' he said. 'Let's drink.' He filled the glasses. 'Are you with us or with them?' he asked Kate and Louise. At the long trestle table, Emily and her friends were having a competition with Mike and *his* friends to see who could eat the most food in the shortest time.

'With you,' said Kate and Louise together. Dad poured them small glasses of champagne.

'Here goes, then,' said Dad. 'To the house and the garden. To Emily's birthday. To Walter, back on his feet again. To the future.' He emptied his glass in one go. Kate sipped suspiciously at hers, and then drank it quickly. The grown-ups began talking all at once, and before long Kate saw Walter's head beginning to nod.

'Would you like to rest?' she asked him.

'I'll tell you what I'd like,' Walter said. 'You get that wheelchair of mine, and take me down to the arbour. I'd like to sit in peace for a bit.'

Kate fetched the wheelchair, and Louise walked with them. Together the girls eased the wheelchair over the two shallow steps and turned it round so that Walter could look out at the garden.

'Grandad,' said Louise. 'When you saw Kate's mum, you thought it was . . .'

'Your grandma. Yes. Just for a moment. She had a dress just like that. But I en't stupid. I knew that couldn't be.' Walter's eyes were closing again. He opened them again briefly, and they looked at Kate, very sharp and clear. 'Louise told me about your mum and dad,' he said. 'I hope that work out. You deserve it.'

Kate looked at Louise. 'I'm sorry,' Louise said. 'I didn't mean to. It just came out.'

'It's OK,' said Kate. 'It doesn't matter. I'm glad.' She felt a smooth furry back brush past her, and saw Pups sidle up to Walter's chair. His tail was between his legs and wagging at the same time. For a second, Kate worried that he would jump on top of Walter. But Pups sat by the old man's side and laid his head on his knee. Walter scratched behind Pups's ear. Louise and Kate walked quietly away.

'Where's Walter?' asked Emily. Her magnificent cake stood on the table. It was in the shape of a garden, with hedges and flowers. In the middle were four candles. It was time for Emily to blow them out.

'Leave him,' said Kate. 'He's asleep.'

'Was that Pups I saw?' said Mrs Fuller anxiously. 'How did he get out?'

'It's OK,' said Louise. 'He's not bouncy at all. Don't worry.'

Emily blew out her candles and they all sang happy birthday. When they had eaten their cake Mrs Fuller said, 'It's been a lovely afternoon, but we must get Dad back to the home in time for his supper.'

'I'll fetch him,' said Kate. She hated the thought of Walter having to go back to the home. He was so peaceful here. As she came closer, she saw that Pups was lying at Walter's feet. Walter was lying back in the chair, smiling. The afternoon sun was falling through the leaves and flowers of the climbing rose, dappling his face. He looked almost like a young man again, like the young man in the photo.

And then Kate was running, running, back towards the house.

Chapter 19

The little church was full. The lane outside was blocked with cars. There were so many people. Kate had seen one old man arriving on a bicycle wearing a heavy tweed suit with bicycle clips around the bottoms of the baggy trousers. A very old lady was playing the small, wheezy organ. Mike sat next to Kate on the long pew. Beside him, Emily was sitting on Dad's lap. And then Mum.

Mum had stayed. No-one had said anything. She just hadn't gone. But Kate knew that this wasn't real. Normal life had stopped when

214

she had found Walter in the garden.

The vicar was saying something about lying down in green pastures. Nothing he said seemed to make any sense. People were moving now. The men in black were lifting the coffin. Louise's mum and dad followed it out of the church, and a ragged procession moved slowly out into the churchyard. The wind caught at Kate's clothes and hair as she came out of the porch. The sun was shining from a blue sky, but there was a chill in the air that reminded her of winter. 'That's come straight from Siberia,' muttered an old man behind her. Kate shivered, and thought of Walter, that first time, outside the house. The day she'd put her trainer through the ice into the puddle. She could still hear him laughing.

All the people had gathered around the grave. There was a small yellow digger nearby, and a sheet of green plastic grass was draped over the heaped-up earth. What was wrong with people seeing the earth? thought Kate. The vicar was speaking again.

'The days of a man are but as grass: he flourishes like a flower of the field; when the wind goes over it, it is gone: and its place will know it no more.'

Kate's eyes blurred with tears. They were lowering the coffin on ropes into the hole. She

215

couldn't look. She turned away and there were the fields, and the wind blowing over them. She walked towards the old, crumbling stone wall. The wind was even stronger here, buffeting her as she stared at the empty sky.

After the funeral, everyone went to Louise's house for drinks. Kate looked around for Louise, but she couldn't see her anywhere. Emily was busy making friends with the old man in the tweed suit. She made friends wherever she went. Mike was eating. There were plates full of food everywhere. Kate went up to Louise's room. She was staring out of the window, and her eyes were red. Across the fields in the churchyard, the yellow arm of the digger rose and fell.

Kate sat on the edge of the bed. There were things she wanted to say, but she didn't know how to begin. She felt as though everything she had worked for was worthless. 'I shouldn't have made him come,' she said.

Louise turned to her, astonishment on her face. 'What do you mean?'

'To Emily's party. He didn't want to. I . . .'

'But he did! It was the best thing that could have happened, don't you see?'

'Everything I touch goes wrong,' said Kate.

Tears were streaming down her cheeks. 'Everything.'

'Kate, stop! That's not true.' Louise knelt on the floor beside her. 'The garden made Grandad so happy. Not just seeing it finished like that. Seeing us working at it. Him helping us. And seeing your dad making the house into a home again. He was so miserable before. So lonely. And I never realized. Not until you came.'

'You really think that's true?' said Kate.

'You know it is. He hated seeing the house empty. He hated seeing the garden like that. And then when Gran died . . .'

'I'm glad he saw it,' said Kate. 'I just wish . . . Why did he have to *die*?'

'But he's still *here*,' said Louise. 'He's there in the garden. All the things he planted. And inside us too. I can never look at a plant without hearing his voice, telling me its name. Look at your hands. Go on. Look at them.'

Kate looked. The backs of her hands were brown, deep brown, from the hours she had spent outside. And the palms were hard and deeply lined. As she gazed at them, her vision began to swim. She remembered Walter showing her his own hands. It seemed like years ago. She could hear his voice. '*You keep*

217

at it and maybe one day you'll have hands like
mine . . . green fingers, see?'

'We could go back,' said Louise. 'Back to the churchyard. On our own.'

'Yes,' Kate said. 'I'd like that. I'll tell Mum.'

The wheat had grown high in the fields. Crossing to the church was like wading through deep water. As they came closer they heard the sound of the digger's engine. 'It's Marty,' Kate said.

Marty stopped work when he saw the girls. The hole was filled. Turves were stacked nearby, waiting to be replaced. Kate saw a shovel leaning against a nearby gravestone. 'We could finish it,' she said to Marty.

'I don't know,' he said. 'There's probably rules.'

'Oh, come on,' said Louise. 'Since when have you cared about rules? You could go and have a drink. You ought to.'

'I suppose you can't do any harm. There's only a few spadefuls there.' He grinned. 'I expect Walter'd be pleased. He never liked these machines.'

Kate picked up the shovel and began to work. It felt real. Far more real than the funeral service. Louise brought the squares of turf that were stacked nearby. 'We could plant things,' said Kate suddenly. 'Bulbs. To grow in the spring.'

'Narcissi,' Louise said. 'There are some called *Cheerfulness*. They smell nice. Grandma liked them too.'

They trampled the turf smooth. The grave was just a green mound.

'It feels right,' said Louise. 'He belongs here.'

Kate looked around at all the other graves. There were Fullers everywhere. 'You're so lucky,' she said. 'Even if you do go away to America. It doesn't matter where you go, you'll always know this is here. I haven't got anywhere like this.'

Louise looked at her. 'Your mum . . . ?' She hesitated.

'You mean, is she coming back?'

'Is she?'

'I want to ask her,' said Kate. 'But I can't. I'm afraid of what she might say.'

After tea, Mum studied Kate's garden diary again; the plans of where plants grew; the beautifully coloured drawings; page after page of careful writing describing everything they had done. 'It's so beautiful,' Mum said. 'I'm proud of you. Really I am. And I bet Walter was too.'

Kate nodded. She had to ask Mum. She had to know. But something was happening. Mum was standing up.

'I can't put it off any longer,' Mum said. 'I really must go and pack.'

'But why . . . ?' began Mike.

Kate pushed back her chair and it clattered to the ground. She fled blindly into the garden. Mum came running after her.

'Kate! Stop! Listen to me . . .'

'Why? I don't want to hear. How can you . . . ?'

Kate was sobbing. Mum caught hold of her and hugged her, hard. 'Just listen will you, Kate. You've got it all wrong. I have to go to London because I have a job to do. I can't simply walk out and let people down. And anyway, that's not what I want. I like my job. It's what I want to do.'

'But I thought . . . you and Dad . . .'

'I'm going to London in the morning, Kate, but I'm coming back on Friday night. I'm going to do what I said I'd do in the beginning. I'll work in London during the week, and I'll be here at weekends. And we'll see how it goes. Things were bad. You know that. They don't just suddenly get right again overnight. But I've missed you all. I've missed you so much.'

Mum hugged Kate even tighter. They stood together, holding each other, and then Mum stood back a little, her hands on Kate's shoulders, looking into her eyes. 'You've changed, Kate,' she said. 'You've changed such a lot. We all have. We can't go back, you know. Not to the way things were before. You wouldn't want to, would you?' Kate shook her head, not trusting herself to speak. 'So, come on,' said Mum. 'Let's go in. I bet Emily's waiting for you to read her a story.' When Kate didn't reply, Mum stroked her hair briefly. The familiar gesture brought more tears to Kate's eyes. Then Mum wasn't there any more.

Kate stood in the garden that she had made. She tried to look into the future, and panic began to take hold of her again. She couldn't see the future at all. All it held was a terrifying emptiness. But what had she been expecting? She knew she'd been stupid to hope that Mum would tell her everything was fine; to hope that there wouldn't be any more Monday mornings or Friday nights; to hope that there wouldn't be any more phone calls. But she *had* hoped. And now . . .

She stood there, rooted to the spot by her fears. And as she stood, the rim of a huge orange moon began to rise, very slowly, over the ripening cornfields. The cold wind of the morning had vanished as quickly as it had come. The air was still, full of smells. Kate became aware of tiny noises – rustlings . . . squeaks . . . a quick flutter of wings as a bird settled to sleep in the hedge. A tiny vole darted across the grass, right at her feet. All around her, things were growing silently.

How could I ever have called this place dead? she thought. She could feel the garden, and everything in it, as if it was a part of her. And more than the garden, the countryside around it, spreading out into the distance under the silver clouds and the stars. This is where I belong, Kate thought, astonished. This is *me*. Not London, not school, not what Mum and Dad want. This.

She walked slowly to the stone bench under the roses, and sat down. Above her head, stars danced among the leaves. She thought about Walter and Louise, about everything that had happened, about Mum and Dad, about the garden. She sat for a long time, long enough for the stars to turn in the sky. Then the door opened, spilling light across the grass.

'Kate,' called Mum, 'Emily's waiting.'

Kate stood up. In the bright moonlight she noticed that weeds were beginning to grow again in the flowerbeds. There was a lot to do.

Tomorrow, she would begin.

THE END